William S. Burke, J. L. Rock, Board of Trade

The History of Leavenworth

the metropolis of Kansas, and the chief commercial center west of the

Missouri River

William S. Burke, J. L. Rock, Board of Trade

The History of Leavenworth
the metropolis of Kansas, and the chief commercial center west of the Missouri River

ISBN/EAN: 9783337293567

Printed in Europe, USA, Canada, Australia, Japan

Cover: Foto ©Andreas Hilbeck / pixelio.de

More available books at **www.hansebooks.com**

THE

HISTORY

OF

LEAVENWORTH,

THE

METROPOLIS OF KANSAS,

AND THE

Chief Commercial Center West of the Missouri River.

THE

Superior Mercantile and Manufacturing Facilities of the City.

BY

W. S. BURKE and J. L. ROCK,

Under the Supervision of the Leavenworth Board of Trade.

LEAVENWORTH, KANSAS:

THE LEAVENWORTH TIMES BOOK AND JOB PRINTING ESTABLISHMENT.

1880.

THE

HISTORY

OF

LEAVENWORTH,

THE

METROPOLIS OF KANSAS,

AND THE

Chief Commercial Center

WEST OF THE MISSOURI RIVER.

THE

Superior Mercantile and Manufacturing Facilities

OF THE CITY.

The Agricultural Advantages of Leavenworth County
Impartially Discussed.

BY

Wm. S. BURKE and J. L. ROCK,

Under the Supervision of the Leavenworth Board of Trade.

LEAVENWORTH, KANSAS:
THE LEAVENWORTH TIMES BOOK AND JOB PRINTING ESTABLISHMENT.

1880.

View of Leavenworth City in 1866.

THE HISTORY OF LEAVENWORTH.

CHAPTER I.

LOCATION.

Leavenworth is situated upon a high plateau, on the west bank of the Missouri river, in latitude 39° 19', and in longitude 94° 58' west from Greenwich, at an average altitude above sea level of eight hundred and fifty feet. The town site is rolling, and furnishes a perfect natural system of drainage ; the inclinations are not sharp enough to cause any steep grades, or to interfere with the use or beauty of the streets, but sufficient to carry the water from all points to the river, and thus to insure the public health against the malarious exhalations from cess pools or ponds of stagnant water, and all the other dangers that unavoidably spring from imperfect drainage. It is surrounded on three sides by a range of hills, at an average distance of two and a-half miles. Starting from the river on the north, these sweep by a graceful curve around the city, on the west, returning to the river again on the south, forming a crescent which encloses the city upon the north, south and west, and completely protects it from the force of the prevailing storms, which nearly always set from one of these three points. It is conceded by all that the town-site of Leavenworth, for health, beauty, comfort and convenience, is one of the best in the world, and is not surpassed by any in the Western States. The peculiar situation of the city, above referred to — within a crescent of high river hills — not only gives to Leavenworth a beautiful and picturesque location, which continually delights the eye, and enhances the comfort of the people, but it gives to the place an almost absolute guarantee against destructive storms. The city is exposed only on the east, and owing to the general conformation of the country, and to certain meteorological laws which it is not necessary here to discuss, severe storms of wind rarely or never come from that direction. Their course is always up or down the valley of the river, or eastward from the mountains, and a storm coming from any one of these three points is met, and the force of the wind broken, by the range of sur-

rounding hills, before it reaches the city. To the great majority of people this is a very important consideration, since
there are but few things incident to climate or locality more
to be dreaded than the terrible wind storms that sometimes
sweep over the great central belt of the American continent
with such destructive force, and the peculiar circumstance of
location which guarantees us immunity from these, is a consideration not to be lost sight of by the person who contem-
plates making his home in the west.

Being in the 39th degree of north latitude, the climate is
temperate, and is free from the objections that are urged
against either extreme ; it is not too far north nor too far
south, but enjoys most of the advantages of the north
and of the south, with very few of the disadvantages of
either. No better apples are raised in Michigan or Vermont, than are produced in Leavenworth county, and within
the same orchard enclosure may be raised peaches and
apricots, such as cannot be surpassed in Texas or Delaware;
winter wheat yields most abundantly of the best quality, and
in the same field may be raised cotton as good as can be produced in Arkansas or Mississippi. All the fruits and vegetables of the temperate zone are raised here in abundance, but
the central location of the place—just between the north and
the south—is perhaps more noticeable in the great variety of
our birds, than in any other particular. Those that are
peculiar to every other section of the country meet here upon
common ground, and at different seasons of the year our ears
are regaled with the music of the birds of every section of the
United States, from east to west, and from north to south;
the hum and whir of the prairie hen mingles with the notes
of the blue jay, and the plain timid song of the wren is
heard at once with the bold and endless variations of the
mocking bird.

The location of the city is particularly favorable to health,
and the mortuary statistics show that the proportion of deaths
is at the minimum, while the general average of the public
health is not higher in any city of equal size in the United
States. Indeed, there is nothing in the location or surround-
ings of the city to generate or aggravate disease— no swamps,
no malarial places, no stagnant water, no imperfect drainage,
in short none of the hundred causes which in most great cities

conspire to breed disease and pestilence, but with a free and unobstructed circulation of pure air, with pure wholesome water, with a congenial climate, and with a market always supplied with healthful fruits and vegetables in generous quantities, and at such low prices that even the poorest persons may always secure an abundance; nature seems to have left nothing undone to encourage and promote the healthfulness of the place, and to reduce the liability of disease to the lowest probable point. Of course we do not mean to have the reader infer that people here are never sick, but the idea we wish to convey is that the very smallest proportion of disease is due to extraneous causes, or causes peculiar to location or climate, over which the patient may have no control. People who live near malaria-breeding swamps or marshes, or in the midst of poisonous gases generated through imperfect drainage, are liable at all times to attacks of most malignant fevers, no matter what precautions they may take against disease, or how carefully they may guard themselves against exposures and indiscretions. But it does not follow that the removal of these causes will prevent all the people from being sick, since the air, the water, and the fruits of Paradise could not keep us always well if we should abuse our systems by dissipation, by exposure, by over eating and poor ventilation. And hence it follows that while all the unavoidable causes of disease above referred to are absent in the case of Leavenworth, our physicians still have enough to do. It must not be inferred, therefore, that because the location is one of the most healthful in the world, and the climatic conditions the most salubrious, that you will never be sick ; but this much you may safely assume — that your chances of continuous good health will be as good here as at any other point upon the American continent, and that your immunity from disease will depend almost exclusively upon your own conduct, and the respect that you show for the laws of health. While we cannot promise you that you shall be always well, we can safely assure you that nature will do her part if you will do yours.

CHAPTER II.

SETTLEMENT.

The City of Leavenworth takes its name from the United States post and reservation of the same name, which was originally known as Cantonment Leavenworth, established by Col. Leavenworth of the Third U. S. Infantry, in May, 1827. The first settlement* was made by a company of persons from Weston, Missouri. The town site was "claimed," or settled upon, by them June 9th, 1854. This company consisted of thirty-two persons, whose names are given elsewhere. This was the first town settlement in the Territory, and consequently Leavenworth justly claims to be the oldest town in the State of Kansas, and from the first has always been the largest town, being the pioneer city of the State, as well as the metropolis.

The town site was located on the "Delaware Trust Lands," as they were called, being a portion of the lands ceded to the United States by treaty with the Delaware tribe of Indians.

The following is a copy of the original paper, taken from the paper itself now before us, and agreed to by the respective parties, whose names are attached, at the time specified.

"ARTICLES OF ASSOCIATON.

" We, the undersigned, being desirous of procuring a claim to a certain tract of land in the Delaware lands, adjoining the military reservation in the Territory of Kansas, with the ultimate view of perfecting a title to the same from the General Government, have caused the same to be regularly and properly laid out and staked off and marked out, with the name of each member, and a registry of the same made with —— Grover, a person appointed by the squatters of the Territory for that purpose, to receive and make such entries or registry. For the speedy furtherance of this object, it is hereby mutually and sacredly agreed between the members of this association, each pledging himself to the other, that we will protect and defend each in all possible ways against all aggression whatsoever, until a title to the same is fully perfected, and it

---

*For all essential facts in regard to the first settlement of Leavenworth the writer is indebted to Hon. H. Miles Moore, secretary of the original town company, and who is still a resident of the city.

is further agreed by and between us that we will hold said tract jointly in common, until a final division of the same may be made by a majority of the members. We further pledge ourselves to furnish the sum of two dollars and fifty cents each for the survey and laying out of said tract, and all other sums that may be assessed by a majority of the members for the purposes of protecting and defending the same from all aggression whatsoever. And we also further pledge ourselves and solemnly promise that we will cordially obey all needful rules and regulations that may be hereafter passed by a majority of this society for the government and protection of its members, upon a no less penalty than that of expulsion from said society, together with the loss of all claim, interest or title in and to said tract above referred to, and all protection from said society, or either of its members, shall thereby be withdrawn. It is further agreed that it shall be optional with George B. Panton, one of our members, to retain and keep for his own use and benefit the quarter section and the improvements now occupied by him, at the price at which the Government may sell the same, in which event he is to lose all interest in this joint stock company. It is further agreed by the members of this society that Major E. A. Ogden shall have full membership and interest in the society although not signing these articles.

"In testimony whereof we have hereunto set our hands, this 13th day of June, A. D., 1854.

"George W. Gist, D. H. Stephens, W. H. Adams, L. A. Wisely, Samuel Norton, Samuel Fernandis, John G. Gist, Edward Mix, Malcolm Clark, Frans Impey, Frederick Starr, Merritt Johnson, G. H. Keller, Wm. G. Caples, H. Miles Moore, Lorenzo D. Bird, L. W. Caples, Oliver Diefendorf, Amos Rees, Wm. S. Murphy, Joseph Murphy, G. B. Panton, Jos. B. Evans, John Bull, James F. Bruner, J. D. Todd, A. Thos. Kyle. Sackfield Maclin, A. E. Ogden. Samuel F. Few."

Of the original thirty members who signed those articles of agreement but eight are now living, as far as is known, as follows: Oliver Diefendorf, Amos Rees, H. Miles Moore, Joseph Murphy, John G. Gist, Jos. B. Evans, A. T. Kyle and Samuel F. Few.

Of the original members three were ministers, four were lawyers, five were doctors, two were printers, eight were far-

mers, one surveyor, four merchants, two army officers and
army clerk. Two other gentlemen were afterwards admitted
as original members of the association, James W. Hardesty
and W. S. Yohe, both of whom are now living and both
farmers.

Thus, says Mr. Moore, in a sketch from which we copy
the law and gospel, brain and muscle, the honest farmer
and shrewd merchant and business man, Esculapius and
Mars, entered into a sacred contract to build a city and
put ducats in their purses. There was a fierce opposition to
the enterprise from its inception, by outside parties, who
wanted to get in, and certain Government officials, who pre-
tended such sincere devotion to the poor Indian, who in their
vivid imagination was being robbed by the avarice of the
squatters, when in truth and in fact had the town company
succumbed to their gentle pressure, for a liberal divide, they
might have bought in their town site at $2.50 per acre instead
of $24.000 for the 320 acres city proper.

Thus it will be seen that Leavenworth commenced her
existence as a city by being made the victim of extortion, and
proper respect for the truth of history compels us to admit
that a very large share of her subsequent experience has been
strikingly consistent with the manner in which she started.

Shortly after the signing of the above articles of agreement, the association met and proceeded to organize, by elect-
ing Gen. George W. Gist president; H. Miles Moore, secretary;
Jos. B. Evans, treasurer; Amos Rees, L. D. Bird and Maj. E.
A. Ogden, trustees. Shortly after a committee of three were
appointed to draft a constitution and by-laws. L. D. Bird, O.
Diefendorf and H. Miles Moore, such committee. The original draft of the constitution is before us, with its erasures
and interlineations, part in Judge Bird's handwriting and the
balance in Mr. Moore's.

Messrs. Bird and Diefendorf, a majority of the committee,
reported in favor of naming the town "Douglas," after Hon.
Stephen A. Douglas, of Illinois. Mr. Moore made a minority
report, favoring the name of Leavenworth, after Fort Leavenworth, arguing that Fort Leavenworth was known all over
the country as one of the most beautiful and eligible sites in
the West, and that one hundred miles distant it would generally be understood that the town was at the Fort. The asso-

ciation adopted the minority report on name, and thus Mr. Moore is entitled to the honor of naming the town.

The original town site, as above stated, contained 320 acres, lying south of the military reservation of Fort Leavenworth, and between that and Three Mile Creek on the south, and extending from the Missouri River (its east boundary) west, so as to include the above named number of acres. It was surveyed and platted by Gen. Gist, and was originally divided into 150 shares, containing twelve lots to the share. Three shares were at first divided to each one of the stockholders and seven retained by the trustees, to be disposed of for the benefit of the town. Afterwards two more shares of twelve lots each were set apart to each original stockholder.

A drawing of two lots to each share was had, so as to give each share a first and second-class lot on either the Levee, Main or Delaware, or Shawnee streets, below Second street. A large number of shares were sold to other parties, who signed the constitution and became members of the association.

Among those who purchased shares were several army officers, then stationed at Fort Leavenworth, some of whom still own property here. Gen. F. E. Hunt, then Captain of the Fourth Artillery, Gen. Magruder, Gen. B. C. Card, then Lieut. Card, Gen. R. C. Drum, then Lieut. Drum, Lieut. Robertson, Dr. Samuel Phillips, Gen. Joseph E. Johnston, and many others.

The Association during the summer of 1854 expended about $4,500 in cutting the timber and brush with which the site was thickly covered. The money was raised by assessment upon the stockholders.

The *Kansas Herald* was the first newspaper printed in the Territory—the first number being issued on the 15th day of September, A. D., 1854, under the "old elm tree," on the Levee, near the corner of Cherokee street and the Levee. It was owned and published by W. H. Adams. The press soon moved into a house, erected by Mr. Adams, on the Levee, the second lot east from Delaware street, where Landis' bakery afterwards stood, the debris of which can still be seen. This was the first building erected in the city. About six weeks after the first publication of the *Herald*, Gen. L. C. Eastin purchased an interest in the same and became editor, and con-

tinued in such capacity up to 1861. Within a few days after
the erection of the Adams' building, Lewis N. Rees built a
store and warehouse attached, on the corner of Delaware and
the Levee, (north side) where P. G. Lowe's building, occupied
by Keith & Co., as a warehouse, now stands.

The next paper to be started in the new town was "The
Kansas Territorial Register, established July 1st, 1855. The
Herald was a pro-slavery organ, but the *Register* was on the
other side; it was a Free-State paper, and was very independent and outspoken. A. M. Sevier was the publisher, and the
late Judge M. W. Delahay, editor. Like most of its successors
in Leavenworth, the *Register* was short-lived, and was
thrown into the Missouri River — type, presses and all — by
a pro-slavery mob, on the night of December 22, 1855.

At the same time "Uncle" George Keller and his son-in-
law, A. T. Kyle, built the house so long known as the "Leavenworth Hotel" — the first hotel in the Territory — on the
corner of Delaware and Main streets, where the Chicago and
Rock Island office now stands. It was in this hotel that Mrs.
J. M. Allen, of this city, and daughter of A. T. Kyle, Esq.,
was born, December 6th, 1854 — the first child born in town.
In front of the hotel, in the street, the first well in the town
was dug and when the street was graded down some thirty
feet, the well was actually dug up.

Capt. W. S. Murphy and Capt. Sim Scruggs, erected
the first saw mill in the country, at the mouth of Three-Mile
Creek, (north side) in the fall of 1854. It stands there now,
and is used as a saw mill to-day. The first dwelling house
was built by Jeremiah Clark, Esq., about the 1st of October,
1854, on the present site of Governor Carney's residence : it
now stands the next house west of the Westminster Church,
on Walnut street. The first church building was erected on
Third street, by Col. H. P. Johnson, near the northwest
corner of Third and Miami streets. A number of buildings
were erected during the summer and fall of 1854. The first
public sale of lots took place on the town site, on the 9th and
10th days of October, 1854. Gen. George W. McLane, in
after years, the editor and publisher of the *Young America*,
and the daily *Ledger*, (the first daily paper published in the
Territory) was the auctioneer. He died at Leadville about the
beginning of the present year—1880.

Fifty-four lots were sold the first day and about the same number the second, at prices ranging from $50 to $350 each — one-third in cash and the other two-thirds when the title was secured. Lot No. 3, Block No. 3, next south of THE TIMES building, was sold to Capt. Grant for $350 — the highest price paid. Whole amount of sales, both days, was $12,000.

The first religious services were held in the town by Elder W. G. Caples, on the bank of the Missouri River, near the reserve line, under the shade of the trees, October 8th, 1854. Shortly after, Father Fish held Catholic services at south side of Shawnee street, near Second. A postoffice was established here in the fall of 1854, and Lewis N. Rees appointed postmaster. The office was in his store, above referred to, corner of the Levee and Delaware street.

The credit of naming the streets after Indian tribes should be given to Major E. A. Ogden, one of the first trustees of the town association, as he suggested to the company as eminently proper that the Indian names should be preserved, and that they were out of the usual style of street names and especially euphoneous. It was so late in the season when the public sale of lots was had, and building material so scarce, that but a limited number of houses were erected in 1854. The next spring the town progressed very rapidly. A large number of houses were constructed during the season — a city soon sprung into being as if by magic. By the next winter the population had reached about 1,200 or 1,500 inhabitants. Several stores, of different kinds, had been opened; also, hotels, boarding-houses, lawyers, and doctors, offices, places of religious worship, saloons and gambling houses. The United States court and its officers, territorial, city and county organizations were in full blast by the close of 1855.

Saturday, the 7th of October, 1854, the steamer "Polar Star," from St. Louis, brought up Gov. Andrew H. Reeder, of Pennsylvania, the first Governor of Kansas Territory. Great preparations had been made to receive him at Weston, Missouri — a little scheme to capture him in advance — but he stopped off at Fort Leavenworth, and so disappointed the Weston boys. Col. A. J. Isaacs, of Alexandria, Louisiana, the newly appointed Attorney-General of the Territory accompanied him. In the afternoon a delegation of citizens waited upon the Governor at the Fort; a very respectable crowd, in numbers at least, had assembled at Capt. Hunt's quarters. Dr. Leib, late of Illinois, but then a citizen of Kansas, addressed the Governor, on behalf of the citizens of the Territory, there assembled. The Governor replied in a neat and happy, but brief speech, after which the champagne flowed generously.

Two of the United States Territorial Judges — Hon. Saunders W Johnson, of Cincinnati, Ohio, and Hon. Rush Elmore, of Montgomery, Alabama, reached here on Tuesday, the 10th of October, 1854. Hon. S. D. Lecompte, the Chief Justice, arrived at Leavenworth a short time after this date.

Gen. John Calhoun, Surveyor-General of Kansas and Nebraska Territories, reached Fort Leavenworth about the 12th of March, 1855, where he first opened his office as Surveyor-General of the above territories. He got some shares out of the town company, by promising to establish his office at Leavenworth, but violated his word. Calhoun also got shares in other towns upon similar promises. He then located his office at Wyandotte, then moved it to Nebraska City, and finally landed at Lecompton. His reputation as President of the Lecompton Constitutional Convention, and manipulator of returns in a candle box, are all familiar to those who have read the political history of those days.

The first Board of County Commissioners for Leavenworth county was composed of John A. Halderman, Probate Judge and *ex-officio* President of the Board ; Joseph Hall, (both of Leavenworth City,) and Mathew R. Walker, of Wyandotte village, then in Leavenworth county. They held their respective positions by virtue of the action of the joint session of the legislative assembly of the Territory of Kansas. The commission of Judge Halderman bears date 27th day of August, A. D., 1855; that of J. M. Hall, the same date; and of Mathew R. Walker, 29th of August, A. D., 1855. They were all issued and signed by Daniel Woodson, acting Governor of the Territory of Kansas, at the "Shawnee Manual Labor School."

The City of Leavenworth was duly incorporated and a special charter granted by the first Territorial Legislature at Shawnee Mission in the summer of 1855. A supplemental act was passed a few days after providing for an election for Mayor and Councilmen, and "appointing J. Harvey Day, W H. Adams, and Lewis N. Rees, of the City of Leavenworth.

for Judges of the election to hold the first election for a Mayor and Board of Councilmen under the provisions of the original act. The time was to be fixed by said Judges and they were to give at least three days' notice of the time and place by ten written or printed hand bills put up at ten public places in said city. They were to give to the Mayor and Council the certificate of their election." The act of incorporation and the supplemental act can be found in the statutes of Kansas of 1855, pages 837 to 847, inclusive, also the two first acts in book of city charters and ordinances of Leavenworth revised and compiled, 1869 and 1870. Although there are quite a number of persons in this city now who must have been present at that election, there are but two persons in this whole section of the country who were city officers at that first election, viz: George Russell, still a resident and stove merchant on Delaware street, south side, between Third and Fourth streets, and William T. Marvin, a farmer in Easton township, in this county, formerly a member of the Board of County Commissioners. They were both elected Councilmen. There is no official record of that election that can be found; although diligent inquiry has been made of many persons, no one yet has been able to fix the precise date of the election. This but shows how rapidly those little items of especial interest to our city's history are being lost. Mr. H. Miles Moore, who then kept and still keeps a daily journal of events, states that his best judgment is, that the election was held on Monday, the 3d of September, 1855, as he reached here from a trip East, on the 5th of September, and that the election had been held a few days before. The first meeting of the City Council was held on Tuesday, the 11th of September, 1855, over J. L. Roundey's furniture store, on Main street, east side, third lot from the corner of Delaware street. It was the day on which the Leavenworth Town Association held a meeting and drew four additional lots to each share. Thos. Slocum was the first Mayor. Dr. J. H. Day, Councilman and President of the Board. The other Councilmen (all elected at large) were Fred Emery, M. L. Truesdell, —— McClelland, Thos. H. Doyle, George Russell, Wm. T. Marvin, Dr. G. J Park and Adam Fisher. After the Board was organized they elected Scott J. Anthony, Register or City Clerk; Wm. A. McDowell, City Marshal—he resigned October 17, 1855, and J. L. Roundey was appointed in his place; William H. Baily, City Treasury; H. G. Weibling, Assessor; John I. Moore,

City Attorney: E. L. Berthoud, City Engineer, now a resident of Colorado, a captain in the late war, and the discoverer of Berthoud's Pass through the Rocky Mountains; M. L. Truesdell, Comptroller.

The first fire company was organized by consent of the City Council September 17, 1855. The first city ordinance passed September 17, 1855, was entitled: " Relating to games of chance and skill."

Of the city officers all are dead except Dr. Day, now in Oregon: Scott J. Anthony, a wealthy citizen of Denver; Fred Emory, George Russell and Wm. T. Marvin now here, and E. L. Berthoud, now of Colorado.

The names and terms of office of those who have filled the general offices of the city from that time to the present, are as follows:

Mayor Slocum resigned his office as Mayor and Wm. E. Murphy was elected to fill vacancy January 21, 1856.

Wm. A. McDowell resigned as City Marshal October 17, 1855, and John L. Roundey was elected in his place to fill vacancy.

John L. Roundey resigned as Marshal January 17, 1856, and William Wood was elected for unexpired term, and resigned February 25, 1856, and George A. Gery was appointed to fill vacancy.

In September, 1856, Wm. E. Murphy was re-elected Mayor.

September 13, 1856, the following city officers were elected by the Council: William Perry, Register or Clerk; James P. Bird, Treasurer; Wm. P. Shockley, City Marshal; Hugh M. Moore, City Attorney.

March 25, 1857, William E. Murphy resigned, and on March 30, 1857, William Perry resigned as Register.

April 1, 1857, John Gill Spivey was elected City Register by the Council.

April 13, 1857, Henry J. Adams was elected Mayor to fill vacancy, occasioned by the resignation of William E. Murphy.

April 20, 1857, J. Gill Spivey, resigned as Register.

April 27, 1857, E. Magruder Lowe was elected Register by the Council.

July 7, 1857, E. Magruder Lowe resigned as Register, and J. C. Green was appointed by the Council in his stead.

September 7, 1857, Henry J. Adams was re-elected Mayor. September 11, 1857, J. C. Green was again appointed City Register.

September 14, 1857, John Kendall was appointed City Marshal, and on the same day John McKee was appointed Treasurer.

September 6, 1858, H. B. Denman was elected Mayor; I. G. Losee, Marshal; J. C. Green, Clerk; John McKee Treasurer; William Stanley, City Attorney.

September 5, 1859, H. B. Denman, was re-elected Mayor; Thomas Plowman, Treasurer; George Einstein, Clerk; Livius Hazen, Marshal; Charles W. Helm, Attorney.

September 3, 1860, James L. McDowell was elected Mayor; Thomas Plowman, Treasurer; George Einstein, Clerk; John McKee, Marshal; H. W. Ide, Attorney.

September 2, 1861, Warren A. Lattin was elected Mayor; Paul Rohr, Treasurer; Otto C. Beeler, Clerk; James Jennings, Marshal; N. H. Wood, Attorney.

April 7, 1862, H. B. Denman was elected Mayor; George R. Hines, Treasurer; Otto C. Beeler, Clerk; James Jennings, Marshal. W. S. Carroll was elected City Attorney by the Council on September 16, 1862.

April 6, 1863, D. R. Anthony was elected Mayor; Thos. Plowman, Treasurer; Henry C. Keller, Clerk; and C. B. Pierce was appointed City Attorney April 9, 1863.

April 4, 1864, J. L. McDowell was elected Mayor; Thomas Plowman Treasurer; Samuel J. Darrah, Clerk; J. Milton Orr, Marshal; and Samuel S. Ludlum was appointed City Attorney April 12, 1864.

April 3, 1865, Thomas Carney was elected Mayor; John Hosick, Treasurer; H. J. Dennis, Clerk; Charles H. Miller, Marshal; and E. Stillings was appointed City Attorney April 20, 1865.

April 2, 1866, Thomas Carney was re-elected Mayor; John Hosick, Treasurer; P. H. Madden was elected Clerk; Joseph Mackle, Marshal; and E. Stillings was re-appointed City Attorney April 10, 1866, and resigned March 26, 1867. Byron Sherry was appointed City Attorney March 26, 1867.

April 1, 1867. John A. Halderman was elected Mayor; John Hosick, Treasurer; H. J. Dennis, Clerk; Joseph Mackle, Marshal; and Willard G. Gambell was appointed City Attorney April 16, 1867.

Mr. Gambell resigned as City Attorney December 10, 1867, and Byron Sherry was appointed City Attorney December 12, 1867.

April 7, 1868, Charles R. Morehead was elected Mayor; Philip Koehler, Treasurer; P. H. Madden, Clerk; H. A. Robertson, Marshal; H. Miles Moore, Attorney.

April 5, 1870, John A. Halderman was elected Mayor; Henry Deckelman, Treasurer; W. W. Creighton, Clerk; H. A. Robertson, Marshal; H. Miles Moore, Attorney.

April 4, 1872, D. R. Anthony was elected Mayor; John Kirch, Treasurer; W. W. Creighton, Clerk; D. A. Hook, Marshal; Lucien Baker, Attorney.

April 7, 1874, J. L. Abernathy was elected Mayor, and on May 22, 1874, A. McGahey was appointed Treasurer; F. P. Fitzwilliam, Attorney; D. A. Hook, Marshal; W. B. Challacombe, Clerk.

F. P. Fitzwilliam resigned his office as Attorney June 16, 1874, and on the same day H. Miles Moore was appointed City Attorney to fill vacancy.

April 6, 1875, Alex. McGahey was elected Treasurer; H. Miles Moore, Attorney; D. A. Hook, Marshal.

April 6, 1876, Fred M. Spalding was appointed Clerk, and the Mayor, under the law, held his office over until the April election in 1877.

April 3, 1877, George Unmethun was elected Mayor; Fred M. Spalding, Clerk; J. H. Gillpatrick, Attorney; Thomas Moonlight, Marshal.

Alex. McGahey was appointed Treasurer April, 1877, and served until July 7, 1877, when he resigned and Geo. D. Farr was appointed Treasurer in his stead.

April 1, 1879, W. M. Fortescue was elected Mayor; Fred M. Spalding, Clerk; Thomas Moonlight, Marshal; E. L. Carney, Attorney.

April 28, 1879, George D. Farr resigned as Treasurer, and on the same day John McKee was appointed Treasurer in his stead.

Fred. M. Spalding held the office of Clerk until August 18, 1879, when he was removed and H. J. Dennis was appointed Clerk in his stead.

All the other general officers elected in 1879 are still serving.

H. J. Dennis was elected Clerk in April, 1880.

During the several terms of Messrs. Denman, Lattin, Anthony and Carney nearly all the public improvements in the city were made. During the period covered by the time these gentlemen occupied the Mayor's office public buildings were erected, streets were graded and paved, sidewalks were constructed, several railroads were completed to the town, and Leavenworth was known as the busiest, most prosperous and most rapidly growing city in the West.

CHAPTER III.

RAPID GROWTH OF THE TOWN.

The growth of Leavenworth was rapid beyond precedent. It sprang into existence as if by magic, and at once assumed a position of prominence and importance. It improved and built up at a rate unparalleled even among the rapidly growing western towns of that time, and when the war of the rebellion commenced—only about six years from the time the town site of Leavenworth was "claimed" and "staked off," it found the place a city, in fact as well as in name, with streets and walks graded and paved, with fine churches, fine school houses, elegant residences, with solid blocks of large and substantial business houses, and with a levee crowded with river steamers, and presenting a scene of life and animation, such as is to be witnessed now only at the docks of important sea port towns. The civil war, which then began to bring demoralization and hard times, or absolute ruin to nearly all the "border" towns and cities of the country, had the opposite effect upon Leavenworth, and stimulated the place to new and more wonderful growth. The horrors of war drove away people and business from the neighboring towns of Missouri, which were subjected to alternate raids from roving bands of soldiers of both contending armies,

2

being pillaged one day by jayhawkers and sacked the next by
bushwhackers. The effect of this, of course, was to utterly
paralyze all kinds of business; not only was trade of all kinds
wholly suspended, but the people were left without any
measure of security for their property or their lives. All
those who could get away, gathered up their movable effects
and fled from the towns referred to, for the purpose of seeking asylum elsewhere. Leavenworth, being situated immediately adjoining the government reservation, and protected
by the guns of the fort, offered a measure of safety to the
citizen which could not be found elsewhere in this portion of
the West, and as a consequence many thousands of those who
had been driven from their homes, by the fortunes of war, in
other places, here found shelter and safety, and went to work
to make new homes. The thousands of troops who were
always at Fort Leavenworth in those days stimulated the retail
trade of the city to a wonderful extent, and this caused the
establishment and maintenance of as many shops and retail
places of all kinds as are usually supported by a city with
twice the population of Leavenworth at that time. The town
grew rapidly. Money was abundant, everybody was busy,
and everybody was prosperous. But, as we have shown,
much of this growth and prosperity was artificial; it had no
solid foundation to rest upon, but sprang from the accidents
of war and the misfortunes of our neighbors, and the causes
of it disappeared with the coming of peace.

When the war ended, and peace was restored, the number
of troops at the Fort was reduced from many thousands to a
few hundreds. This immediately cut off nearly one half the
trade upon which the numerous retail shops had lived—for
the soldiers were liberal customers—and the restoration of
law and order gave security to the neighboring towns, which
immediately went to work to repair the wastes of war, and to
recover their lost business. Their trade, which for four years
had been driven to Leavenworth by the force of circum-
stances, began to come back to them, and many of their citizens who had sought refuge with us began to return to their
homes. The effect of this condition of things, upon Leavenworth, can be readily understood, without any explanation.
The fortunes of war had caused her to flourish at the expense
of her neighbors, and had forced upon her an artificial hot-
house growth, far beyond the natural demands of the coun-

try, and when the causes which had led to this were removed she began to have her first experience with "hard times." She had hundreds of shops more than the natural demands of the country could support, and when the extraordinary trade upon which these had grown up was withdrawn, their keepers were obliged to seek a livelihood in other channels of employment, and large numbers of them drifted to other towns. The city entered upon a period of depression, extending over several years. It had been built to a large extent upon an inflated and fictitious basis, far beyond the demands of the country surrounding it; indeed, at that time, one-fifth of the entire population of the State was within the corporate limits of Leavenworth; the town had grown to be a great city, in the midst of a State which was yet comparatively without business and without people, and when the extraordinary conditions upon which it had thriven and grown were removed, and it was obliged to depend upon the natural and legitimate demands of the country tributary to it, there was nothing to do but to stand still and wait. The town had grown far beyond the demands of the country, and it was now compelled to wait for the country to grow up to it. This caused improvements to stop, caused business to languish, and soon gave the once growing, rushing city the reputation of a "dead town."

And this condition of things was aggravated by the fact that the sole dependence of the place had hitherto been upon commercial interests: buying and selling goods was the sole business of the town. This was entirely satisfactory so long as the war continued, and all the people in this part of the country were forced to come to Leavenworth to buy, but with the close of the war, and the resumption of business in neighboring towns, the people of those vicinities went back to their old markets. The railroad system of the West also at that time began to be developed, and country dealers began to send their orders direct to St. Louis, Chicago, and New York. Up to this time there were no railroads reaching Kansas from the east. All our merchandise was brought by steamers up the Missouri River, and the mammoth warehouses of the wholesale dealers of Leavenworth were the depots of supplies for not only all of Kansas but for Colorado and New Mexico. The building of railroads to the Missouri Valley and into Kansas, which occurred almost simultaneously with the close of the war, served to revolutionize the commercial system of the country; 'the steamboat's mission was accomplished, and it was driven from the river by the railroad, as the buffalo and the Indian were driven from the land by the white man. There was no longer a necessity for a grand depot of supplies at the bank of the river, for the goods loaded into the car at St. Louis or Chicago, could be carried on to Topeka or Emporia just as well as to Leavenworth, and by going through direct would save the expense of handling.

This changed condition of affairs rendered it necessary for Leavenworth to look to other avenues of business. Hitherto she had lived solely upon her commerce, and many of her merchants had amassed princely fortunes, but the changes in the current of trade, wrought by the development and extension of the vast railroad systems of the West, cut off, to a large extent, this source of wealth, and the rich trade which up to this time had all centered at this place, was now diffused and scattered to dozens of different points, going mainly to the great cities of the East. Manufactures, up to this time, had received little or no attention. Everbody had been able to make money so rapidly by simply handling and exchanging goods, that nobody had any time or inclination for the slow processes of production. There was little or nothing manufactured in the place, and while the region surrounding the city was one of the finest wheat growing districts on the continent, and its grain was quoted at the highest figures in the market, even the very bread upon which the people lived was made of flour manufactured by the mills of Missouri and Illinois. Then it was that the public attention began to turn toward manufactures. Our people began to realize the fact that while we had expended millions to build up a great city, we had not expended a dollar in preparing a foundation for it to stand upon. We had called together more than twenty thousand people : we had built them good homes to live in, fine churches to worship in, elegant school-houses in which to educate their children : we had given them theaters and halls in which to seek amusement and instruction : we had given them fine streets, lined with magnificent stores, and lighted with gas ; we had provided in short, for giving them everything but employment ; we had given them the most beautiful, the most healthful and the most attractive city in the West to live *in*, but we had given them nothing on earth to live *on;* we had provided everything but the one all-essential thing—employment. And when the trade which had been driven from other towns by the war began to go back to them, and the railroads began to carry their freight to the interior of the State, we had our eyes painfully opened to the unwelcome fact that we had builded without a foundation ; that we were a city without business, and a people without employment.

<hr />

CHAPTER IV.

DEVELOPMENT OF MANUFACTURES.

It was very plain to everybody that the people of Leavenworth must turn their attention to some new channels of business. Hitherto they had lived by selling goods to their neighbors, and by building houses for one another, but as we have said in the foregoing chapter, the great changes that had taken place in the commercial character of the country, simultaneously with the close of the war, had put a stop to the selling of goods to a very large extent, and the work of building houses was already overdone. It was very plain that we could not long keep thousands of mechanics employed in building new houses, unless we could furnish occupants for the houses when they were done, and this we could not hope to do unless we were prepared to furnish some means of employment for the people. . To do this it was clearly apparent that we must turn our attention to manufacturing. Cities, in this country, have only two great means of support—commerce and manufactures. The development of the great railroad systems of the West, together with our own experience, had abundantly demonstrated the fact that commerce was destined to be concentrated at a few great trade centres, and that no inland town could reasonably hope to make a great permanent growth upon a commercial basis, hence the attention of our people was turned toward manufacturing. As we looked about us we saw a great and rapidly growing population ; we saw a State soon destined to be an Empire within itself ; extending from Nebraska to the Indian Territory, and from the Missouri River to the base of the Rocky Mountains; possessing within itself the " promise and potency" of sustenance, livelihood and competence for not only thousands but millions of people; a State as great in area as all of New England, and as great in its producing capacity as a dozen New England's; and we saw that up to this time no single step had been taken toward the necessary work of manufacturing the millions of dollars' worth of articles of use and luxury which every year would be demanded to supply the wants of the hundreds of thousands of people who were destined soon to settle up our vast and fertile plains, and who even then were coming. Here, then, was a field of industry that was not occupied — a field that contained a mine of untold wealth ; a field that lay with its whole broad promise before us, and we had only to "go up and possess the land."

The people of Leavenworth then turned their attention seriously and earnestly toward the work of establishing manufactories. They put their own money freely into such enterprises, and lost no opportunity to encourage foreign capital to invest among them. One after another, establishments of various kinds were started, and the experience of all was the same, and was to the effect that manufacturing was profitable. During the ten years following the close of the war, a large number of manufacturing enterprises were engaged in, all small at first but all meeting with success from the start, and growing rapidly in magnitude and profitableness. To such an extent did the manufacturing interests of the city develop during this period that it soon became evident that some means must be provided for furnishing a readier supply of fuel, and the work of sinking a shaft for coal, (commenced some years before and abandoned for want of capital,) was resumed, and pushed forward to completion. Competent geologists had declared, upon evidence that seemed to be satisfactory, that this portion of Kansas was underlaid with valuable deposits of coal, and that we only had to dig down to these to secure an abundant and unfailing supply of cheap fuel for all the manufactories we might start. The work had been commenced, as stated above, some years before, but had been abandoned before the coal beds were reached, for want of funds. In 1868, the rapidly increasing demand for fuel for manufacturing purposes making it apparent that a coal mine here would be profitable, the company was re-organized, and the work pushed rapidly forward to completion. Coal was found after about a year's work, and it proved to be of excellent quality and in abundance. This gave a fresh impetus to the already rapidly growing manufacturing industries of the place, and not only encouraged those already engaged in such enterprises to enlarge and extend their facilities, but capitalists from abroad, seeking for investment in such lines, were convinced that this was a desirable point. The location of the town, as the entrepot of the great State lying behind it; its ready communication with all parts of the world by railroad, together with the advantage of a navigable river for the transportation of heavy freights, were all strong arguments, and needed only to be supplemented by the one now supplied — an abundance of cheap fuel. This furnished the one thing lacking to insure the permanent success of the place as a manufacturing center, and that being supplied, there was no longer a doubt in the minds of any of her people, as to Leavenworth's future destiny, as the manufacturing center of the Missouri Valley. Then it was that the town began to lay a new and sure foundation of growth and prosperity, and to build upon a basis that was durable and reliable—one that could not be seriously effected by the changing policies of railroads, or the shifting currents of population. The people saw that here was a foundation upon which they could build without fear of being undermined, and they went to work with a will.

From the feeble beginning, made only a little more than a decade ago, the manufacturing industries of Leavenworth have increased and developed, grown and multiplied till the city is now everywhere recognized as the manufacturing center of the Great West, and occupies the same relation to the States west of the Mississippi that Pittsburg occupies to the Middle States. Centrally located, in the midst of one of the richest and grandest agricultural districts in the world, with ready communication with all parts of the country by rail and by river, with an abundance of fuel, good and cheap, at our doors, with produce of every kind so abundant and cheap that the laborer can save money upon the same wages that would barely permit his Eastern competitor to live—all these advantages combine to give Leavenworth facilities in the manufacturing line which are rarely equalled, and which are not surpassed by any point, east or west. And a fair presentation of these facts cannot fail to convince any sensible man who is looking for an opportunity to invest his capital in manufacturing, that Leavenworth gives him the promise of a better return than any other point in the West. The establishments already in operation here have, by the cheapness and superiority of their products, built up a reputation for the city as a manufacturing center, and this reputation is worth just as much to the new establishment that may be started to-day as to those that were the pioneers in the work; for when a town becomes celebrated for its manufactures the articles it produces are sold by the name of the town, and not by the name of the individual, or firm producing them. Pittsburg has a reputation for glass; Wheeling for nails; Louisville for tobacco; Milwaukee for beer, and scores of other towns we might name which, though manufacturing great varieties of goods, have gained special prominence in the production of certain lines, and the general public inquires no further than to ascertain the fact that the article was manufactured at that town. If you want to buy a box of glass, or a keg of nails, the brand of Pittsburg, or Wheeling satisfies you that the article is good; you do not stop to inquire the name of the particular firm, and even if you should be told, there is not one chance in a hundred that you would know whether the house was established last week or was one of the pioneers that made the reputation of the town.

Hence it will be seen that Leavenworth is not only the manufacturing center of the new West but that it offers better advantages to those seeking for locations in this line of business than any other point west of the Mississippi, because its facilities for manufacturing are superior to those of any rival town, and because it has already built up a reputation for the superiority of its manufactures which causes its goods to find a ready sale in all the markets of the country.

CHAPTER V.

FINANCIAL.

As a money centre and the grand central base of supplies for the vast West and Southwest, the financial importance of Leavenworth during the war, and for many years thereafter, excelled that of most cities of five times its population. When the civil war closed, therefore, and on to the period of the panic of 1873, there were eight institutions doing a banking business in Leavenworth, each representing some capital, that aggregated about $800,000, and carrying a daily deposit account of $1,500,000.

But, as a spirit of depression and gloom, gradually widening, permeated the entire country, and a season of drouth and failure of crops in Kansas was shortly followed by the terrible grasshopper scourge on her prairies; some of these institutions sank to infantile weakness and ultimately closed.

When, however, in the year 1873, the various premonitory rumblings and warnings were supplemented by the disastrous financial panic, the feebler of the remaining banking houses of Leavenworth succumbed to the inevitable, and *failed*, while others, seeing nothing but disaster in a prolonged continuance, wound up their affairs and retired.

For years after the panic, owing to the great shrinkage of values and the unsettled state of the national finances, there was not a plethora of money in any of the banks of the country, but, happily, that time is past.

The three surviving banks indicated, the First National Bank, the German Bank and the banking house of Insley, Shire & Co., are now doing a better business than at any other time for years. The steady growth of the business interests of Kansas, the accumulation of live stock, and the building of railroads and towns contributed to create a constant increase of floating capital, and the resumption of specie payment has restored unlimited confidence to the holders of money. The three banks named, while having a nominal capital of $350,000, possess the ability to increase at pleasure. Their daily deposits average $1,600,000. Additional to this it is worthy of mention that over $750,000 have been withdrawn from circulation by depositors and converted into United States Government bonds.

The City of Leavenworth is taxed on property valued by the Assessors, at $3,300,000. The rate of taxation for last year for all City purposes was 2.05 per cent., and the total rate for the State, County, School and City purposes was 3.55 per cent. on the assessed value.

The actual value of the property of the City of Leavenworth is near seven millions of dollars, and the rate of taxation on the *real* value of all property for every purpose would be 1.77 per cent. The total amount of tax for all purposes at last assessment in the City was $95,964.

Taxes in Kansas are levied by the State Legislature for State purposes, by the Boards of County Commissioners for County purposes, and by the Boards of Education for School purposes, and by the City Council for City purposes. All these are duly returned to the County Clerk, by him figured, added and placed on the general tax roll. On the first day of November of each year, when taxes become due by law, the County Clerk turns the tax rolls over to the County Treasurer for collection.

Half of the tax is payable by December 20, the other half not payable until the 20th of June of the next year; but if a tax-payer chooses to pay all his taxes prior to December 21st, he receives a rebate of five per cent. on one-half. On December 21st, a penalty of five per cent. is added to the first half of the taxes if not paid, and, if still remaining delinquent, an additional penalty of five per cent. is added, respectively on the 21st days of March and June following, making a total penalty of fifteen per cent. All property on which taxes are unpaid until the second Tuesday of September is sold by the County Treasurer, and thereafter bears twenty-five per cent. interest. In three years from date of sale a purchaser of property at a tax sale is entitled to a deed of the property.

Owing to the very judicious management of the Mayor and Council in bonding the City's scrip, and compromising the city's indebtedness at forty cents on the dollar, by issuing new thirty year bonds bearing five per cent. interest, Leavenworth's taxes hereafter will be lighter each year. A rigid economy, and a determination to pay cash for everything, has replaced the old-time profligacy of extravagance with a business like and thrifty management, restored general confidence and educated the tax-payers to the knowledge that a city's affairs can be run with the same system that characterizes the transactions of private business.

PUBLIC DEBT.

The following is a statement of the public debt of the City, as shown by the annual exhibit made by the City Clerk up to the 31st of March, 1879, and which represents the indebtedness at the present time. with the exceptions noted hereafter.

Bonds bearing 7 per cent. interest,	$ 5,370
Bonds bearing 7 per cent. interest. being Missouri River Railroad Bonds,	209,500
Bonds bearing 10 per cent. interest,	1,700
Bonds bearing 10 per cent. interest, being Mount Muncie Cemetery Bonds,	10,000
Missouri River Railroad Compromise Bonds, 7 per cent	600
Missouri River Railroad Compromise Bonds, 6 per cent	24,900
Installment and Interest Bonds, series " A," 7 per cent	37,395
Installment and Interest Bonds, series " B," 10 per cent	139,840
Old Scrip outstanding, issued prior to April 1st, 1878,	213
New scrip issued. which has either not been called for or the ownership being in dispute is now in the hands of the City Clerk,	2,462
Certificates of indebtedness for bonds and scrip over amount bonded,	974
Certificates on sinking fund for balance of Missouri Railroad Bonds compromised.	425
Total,	$433,291

Under the provisions of Chapters 50 and 55, Laws of Kansas, 1879, authorizing and empowering cities to refund and compromise their indebtedness. active efforts have been made by the Mayor and Council during the past year to refund the outstanding indebtedness at 40 per cent. of the face thereof. by the issue of new bonds bearing 5 per cent. interest, payable semi-annually.

During the past year $89,000, in round numbers. of the above-mentioned indebtedness, has been compromised at 40 per cent. of the face, resulting in a reduction of the public debt of the City to the amount of $58,000, in round figures. All current expenses are now paid from current receipts, not a dollar's worth of work of any kind is done till the money is on hand to pay for it, and no orders are drawn upon the Treasury till the funds are there with which to redeem them. This policy of doing the public business upon a cash basis. and paying as we go, enables the city to reduce its current expenses very considerably, and this, of course, results in a corresponding reduction of taxation. As no new obligations have been incurred during the past fiscal year, the public debt has been reduced by the gross amount of the sum saved through the compromise of bonds, and is, therefore, at the present time, as follows :

Total public indebtedness, of all kinds, as above,.......... $433,291 00
Total reduction by compromise, during 1879,.............. 58,000 00
                                                          _____
Total present indebtedness, ... $375,291 00

The work of compromising the bonds is still going on in a very encouraging manner. The present city officers recognize the importance of having the debt brought down to the minimum at the very earliest day, and are therefore devoting themselves earnestly to the task of settling with our creditors. It is estimated that after making liberal allowance for all the expenses of compromising the present indebtedness will be reduced by not less than $150,000, and this would leave the total public debt at $225,000. This, though a considerable sum, would not be regarded as an onerous burden, and the City, with its present population, wealth and resources, could carry and provide for such an amount of public indebtedness, without crippling its energies or overtaxing its people.

CHAPTER VI.

RELIGIOUS.

All the numerous religious denominations are represented in Leavenworth, all have organized societies and nearly all have commodious houses of worship, some of which are elegant and costly. The largest and most expensive building is owned by the Catholics—the Cathedral of the Immaculate Conception—built at a cost of $200,000, and with seats for 2,000 persons. Next in order of value is the First Baptist Church, costing $60,000, and with seats for 800. Then we have the German Catholic Church, costing $45,000, with accommodations for 800; the Westminster Presbyterian Church, costing $35,000, and accommodating 700; the First Presbyterian Church, costing $25,000, with seats for 600 persons; the First Methodist Church, built at a cost of $24,000, with accommodations for 600; St. Paul's Episcopal Church, costing

$24,000, with seating accommodations for 600; First Congregational Church, costing $20,000, and accommodating 500; First African M. E. Church, costing $16,000, and with seats for 1,000; First Christian Church, built at a cost of $15,000, and with seats for 400; and in addition to these there are seventeen other smaller edifices, namely: Jewish Synagogue, United Presbyterian, Free Methodist, Colored Methodist, German Lutheran, German Evangelical, St. John's Episcopal Chapel, Mission Congregational, Quaker, Colored Catholic, and four Colored Baptist. These range in value from $700 to $9,000, and with seating capacities varying from 150 to 500. The total average attendance at all the churches in the City is 5,900; total membership, 5,370; total seating capacity, about 10,900, and the total cost of all church buildings, $675,000, and the total church indebtednes is only $8,510. Of this sum the Protestants owe $3,610, and the Catholics $4,900. The Protestant portion of the indebtedness is exclusively among the Colored societies.

CHAPTER VII.

EDUCATIONAL.

No city in any of the Western States has better school facilities than Leavenworth. Her educational institutions are the pride of her people. Many young persons from abroad come here to be educated, because of the superiority of our schools, public and private. The Leavenworth public schools are graded upon the same system which obtains in Cleveland, St. Louis, Cincinnati, and other Eastern cities. Great attention is given to primary work, much stress being laid upon writing, reading, and arithmetic. Script writing is commenced immediately upon the entrance of the child into school—usually about the age of six. Pen and ink work begins at the age of seven, or after the child has completed his first year's work in school. In reading great prominence is given to correct expression, accurate enunciation and articulation. Sight-reading is cultivated by the use of supplementary books, magazines, other reading, etc. It is believed that there are few schools able to show more satisfactory primary work; the usual division into Primary. Grammar, and High-School obtains. The 3,000 pupils enrolled are distributed as follows: High-School. 160; Grammar Schools, 600; Primary Schools. 2,240. The High-School course is four years, and pupils find little difficulty in entering Harvard with no other preparation than is obtained within its class-rooms. The government in the school-room is mild but firm, preventive rather than coercive. The control of the schools is vested in a Board of Education, consisting of twelve members, three members from each ward. Members hold their office for three years, one-third retiring each year. The schools are purely secular, no religious instruction whatever being given. Bible, without note or comment, was read until 1874, at which time it was omitted.

The private schools consist of the usual parochial schools of the Catholic Church, having an attendance of about 380; a convent (St. Mary's Academy), under the auspices of the same church; a select German school, having some 100 pup'ls in attendance; and numerous smaller schools, partaking more or less of the Kindergarten character.

There are six public school buildings, all of brick, erected at a total cost of $150,000, and having accommodations for 4,000 pupils. There are nine private school buildings, four of brick, four frame and one stone, built at a total cost of $125,-000. St. Mary's Academy is the most important of the private school buildings, and is a fine brick structure, erected at an expense of $90,000. All the others are small and unimportant.

MORRIS PUBLIC SCHOOL BUILDING.

BANKS AND BANKING IN LEAVENWORTH.

There are three banking houses in Leavenworth which in point of age and reputation, rank among the largest and best institutions of the kind in the Western States. The paid up capital of these banks aggregates $350,000; surplus, $180,000, with an average deposit account of $1,675,000.

THE FIRST NATIONAL BANK.

The oldest National Bank in Kansas, has a paid up capital of $100,000. and was chartered in 1864. Its surplus is $80,000, and its average deposits $1,100,000. In no instance has the check of a depositor left its counter unpaid since the day it opened its doors to the public. It has studiously avoided the quicksands of speculative enterprises that have swallowed up so many banking houses during the past sixteen years, and to-day it enjoys the confidence of the public as the safest and best managed bank in the State. Its management consists of Lucien Scott, President; Lyman Scott, Vice President; Cashier, J. M. Graybill, and Assistant Cashier, George Van Derwerker. all gentlemen of experience and high standing in financial circles. We should have mentioned before that it is one of the Government depositories. The First National owns their bank building, a fine stone front structure, on the northeast corner of Fourth and Delaware streets. On the opposite corner of the above named streets is located the

GERMAN BANK,

Which was organized in 1875, and has a paid up capital of $100,000 and an average deposit account of $275,000. This too, by an upright business career during the five years it has been in operation, has fairly earned the confidence of the public. and deservedly enjoys the reputation of being judiciously managed, reliable and safe. There the funds of depositors are never put in jeopardy by outside speculations. In 1878 the old and well-known banking house of Clark & Co., consolidated with the German Bank; Mr. M. E. Clark being at the present time President, John F. Richards, Vice President, George H. Hyde, Cashier, and Charles Peaper, Assistant Cashier. These gentlemen are all old and reliable citizens of Leavenworth, who have for many years past made the commercial advancement of the City only secondary to their own interests.

THE BANKING HOUSE OF INSLEY, SHIRE & CO.,

Established in 1872, is the second oldest bank in Leavenworth, and in point of capital the first, The firm is composed of M. H. Insley and Daniel Shire, with Wm. H. Carson as Cashier. Messrs. Insley and Shire were among the very first settlers of this city, having lived here for the last twenty-three years, and there are few, if any, that are more largely interested, or that are more prominently identified with the growth and prosperity of the City and State than these gentlemen. The large hotel to be built this season, on the corner of Fifth and Shawnee streets, is an enterprise of Mr. M. H. Insley. This bank has a *paid up capital* of $150,000; surplus, $20,000, and an average deposit account of $250,000. It stands high in financial circles both at home and abroad, and its patronage like all other business interests in the City is largely increasing. It buys and sells exchange and makes collections on all parts of this country and Europe. Thus, it will be seen that Leavenworth has solid banking houses that have never struck their colors to hard times or panics.

THE BENCH AND BAR OF LEAVENWORTH.

This work would be incomplete, and the authors would be liable to the charge of stupidity, should they omit mentioning the Bench and Bar, and while the space at our command will not admit of a personal notice of each member, it is proper to state, that omissions made are not because those not mentioned may not be entirely worthy, for, without any desire to flatter, we will say that the Bar of Leavenworth — for ability, character, and general reputation — ranks second to that of no other in the State.

The Bench.

The United States Circuit Court is presided over by Ex-Secretary of War, George W. McCrary, of Iowa, successor to Judge Dillon, resigned.

The Bench in the United States District Court, for the District of Kansas, is occupied by the Hon. C. G. Foster, of Topeka, who was appointed by Gen. Grant, during his last term.

Judge Albert H. Horton, of Topeka, occupies the Bench of the Supreme Court of the State, with Judge Valentine, of Topeka, and Judge D. J. Brewer, of this City, as Associate Justices.

The District Court of Leavenworth County, is presided over by Judge Robert Crozier, the Probate Court of Leavenworth County, by Oliver Diefendorf, and the Police Court of Leavenworth City, by J. C. Vaughan.

The Bar.

WM. M'NEILL CLOUGH,

a prominent member of the bar of this city, of which he has been a citizen since 1862, has followed his profession since 1854. He is a graduate of the Cambridge (Massachusets) Law School. He is a cautious, studious gentleman, and his opinions command general respect among his associates. He has a large practice, both in the State and National Courts; also, an extensive commercial practice. He has one of the largest law libraries in the City or State. In short, he is a thorough-read lawyer, and is held in high esteem both as a citizen and in his profession.

In speaking of Leavenworth and its present and future prospects, he said: "Leavenworth is on the mend, and I, for one, do not now recollect of a man who has attended strictly to his business, that has not prospered here in Leavenworth. The manufacturing interests are now, and will continue to be an element of importance in building up the city, and as the advantages we possess in that particular become more generally known, that industry must necessarily expand."

C. F. W. DASSLER,

a young lawyer of ability, came to this city from St. Louis, in 1863, although he has been a resident of Kansas since 1868. In the management of cases entrusted to him he has exhibited a breadth of legal ability that has commanded the respect and esteem of the older members of the bar of the City and State. In 1864, Mr. Dassler compiled the first Digest of Kansas Reports; in 1876, Dassler's Kansas Statutes; in 1879, Laws of Kansas — authorized by an act of the Legislature; in 1880, a new Digest of Kansas Reports.

H. MILES MOORE,

was born September 2, 1826, in Brockport, N. Y. He obtained his education under a good many difficulties — losing his parents at an early age. He read and was admitted to practice in Rochester, N. Y., in the same class with Clarence A. Seward, Augustus Van Buren, and others. Commencing practice in 1848, in Louisiana, he remained there until 1850, when he removed to Platte County, Missouri, where he continued practice, and was connected with the *Western Reporter*. He removed to Kansas in 1854, and was one of the original proprietors of Leavenworth, and Secretary of the Town's Company. He was three terms in the legislature, served several years as City Attorney for Leavenworth, and now holds the position of Secretary of State Democratic Committee, of which party he is an active member. Although formerly a slave owner, he served three years in the Union army, and has always been a friend to the Free State cause Mr. Moore is a forcible speaker, a man of good address, and always "ready for the fray in the cause of right." He became a master mason in 1852, and was one of the incorporators of Lodge No. 2, A. F. and A. M., of which he is still a member. He still controls a large general law practice, and is esteemed by all good citizens, and by the Episcopal Church, of which he is an active member.

N. H. WOOD,

was born in New York, and educated at Union College, in Schenectady, N. Y., mainly under the tutelage of the late venerable Dr. Elephalett Nott. Studied his profession and was admitted to the bar in Wisconsin, in 1858. Came to Leavenworth in March, 1859, and entered actively into the practice. Mr. W held the office of Justice of the Peace under the Territorial government, and soon after the admission of Kansas as a State, he was elected to the office of City Attorney, which he filled with credit for one term, and afterwards served as deputy. He was Judge of the Police Court of this city, in 1874-75. He compiled a complete abstract of the Land Records of Leavenworth City and County, and for years gave much of his attention to the Real Estate business, but recently, he has been more devoted to the practice of his profession. He is now, and for upwards of three years last past has been, the Deputy County Attorney, and all things pertaining to that office will be cheerfully attended to by him.

OLIVER DIEFENDORF,

now Judge of Probate, is a native of New York State. He came to Springfield, Ills., in 1840, and was assistant engineer during the building of the then known "Springfield & Meredosia Railroad" Afterwards reading law with Messrs. Stewart & Edwards, he was admitted to the bar in 1845. At the breaking out of the Mexican War, he was commissioned Second Lieutenant of the 4th Regiment of Illinois Volunteers. He served through the war, during which time he was transferred to the 16th Regiment of U. S. Infantry. At the mustering out of his regiment, he was tendered, and accepted, a clerkship in the Land Department at Washington. In 1850, he turned his face westward again, and arrived in Platte County, Missouri, in August, of the same year. He was one of thirty-two original prospectors of the City of Leavenworth, and became a resident of Kansas in 1856. He has held the office of County Clerk for ten years, and was elected to the office of Judge of Probate in 1878. Mr. Diefendorf has had a large and varied experience, and is, and always has been fully identified with the best interests of the city.

THOMAS P. FENLON,

another prominent member of the Bar, came to this city from Pennsylvania, in 1857. He has the reputation of being one of the best and most successful criminal lawyers in the West. He has filled the position of County and District Attorney; was a member of the State Legislature three times, and Speaker — the only Democratic Speaker ever elected — one term He was nominated for Congress in 1876.

T. A. HURD,

Attorney for the Missouri Valley Life Insurance Company, and Local Attorney for the Union Pacific and Missouri Pacific Railroads, has followed his profession here since 1857. He was formerly from Ithica, New York, where he was admitted to the Bar. He is a careful, sound lawyer, and is esteemed by the Bar of both City and State.

MANN & MANN,

307 Delaware street. The above-named law firm is composed of the Mann Brothers, the oldest of whom came to Leavenworth from Delaware County, Ohio, in 1868, graduating from the Western University of that State. He was admitted to practice in Kansas in 1869 He held the office of Probate Judge from 1876 to 1879. Mr. Nathan J. Mann, the younger of the firm, came from Columbus, Ohio, in 1877. He is a graduate of Anterbein Literary University, and also of the Law School of the University of Michigan — class, 1877

They command a large general commercial practice in all the courts, and have conducted a large number of important criminal cases.

L. HAWN.

another esteemed member of the Leavenworth Bar, first came to this city in 1860. He received his legal education at Cornell University, from which he graduated in 1875. He went to Salt Lake City in 1876, where he was admitted to practice in the United States Court. In 1878, he returned to this city and opened an office on Delaware street, and by close attention to and careful management of the business entrusted to him, he has earned a good reputation, and secured a lucrative practice in all of the courts — State and National.

WILLIAM DILL,

who studied law and was admitted to practice in Ohio, came to this city in 1869. During 1871-2 he was Deputy County Attorney, the duties of which position he discharged in a most credible manner. He is a studious, unassuming gentleman, who, by industry and careful management of the business placed in his hands, has acquired a good reputation both as a lawyer and citizen, and earned a fair practice in all the Courts — State and National.

HENRY WOLLMAN,

who made his first appearance at the Bar of this City about two years since, received his legal education at the Law University of Michigan, where he was admitted to practice some six months before he had reached his twentieth year. After his admission to the Bar, he came directly to this city, and was immediately appointed Deputy City Attorney, a position which he filled in a manner that commanded the respect and commendations of the older members of the Bar. He is a young gentleman of ability, and although one of the youngest members in the profession, as an advocate and counsellor, he has shown himself to possess that metal of which our best lawyers are made.

O. N. M'NARY.

a Justice of the Peace and Notary Public, is one of the oldest citizens of this city, and is held in high esteem as a gentleman of business worth and integrity He is at the present time, and has been for the last fourteen years, agent for some of the most solid and reliable insurance companies at the East.

GROVER & HACKER.

Mr. Grover, the senior member of the firm, came here from Kentucky, among the very earliest settlers of Kansas. Although born in Kentucky, he is of the old New England blood — his parents removing from there at an early date. He was State's Attorney during the border days, and some of the important cases for treason were tried at Lecompton — then the Capitol of the Territory during that time and were conducted by him. Mr. Hacker, the junior member of the firm, also came from Kentucky, read law and was admitted to practice here. They control a fair general practice.

THE KANSAS WAGON MANUFACTURING COMPANY.

A VISIT TO THEIR FACTORY BY THE AUTHOR.

So much has been said and written relating to this company and the system upon which they manufacture their famous wagons, and the important relation the industry sustains towards the City and State, that one cannot expect to say anything new or interesting, at least to Western people, with whom the Kansas wagon is as familiar as household words. To the people of the East and of Europe, however, into whose hands this work may fall, we may say something that will prove valuable. The Kansas wagon is a product to which the people of the State may well feel proud. In its manufacture an immense capital is employed, and the scope of its usefulness is broader than that of any other industry in the State. In every State west of the Mississippi these wagons are used, and their superior qualities appreciated. Their light running farm wagon is no more highly prized by the farmer than are their Rocky Mountain freight wagons by the teaming interests of the Pacific States, or their Leadville quartz wagons—double tired, eight tons capacity—are to the freighters of Colorado, Arizona and New Mexico. Or, in other words, the Kansas wagon is as widespread in its usefulness throughout the West as are the railways, and only secondary to them in its relations to the agricultural industries. While they make a specialty of the light running farm wagon they have an extensive patronage from the Government in the way of army wagons, Doughty spring wagons and ambulances. They have just completed an order for two hundred Government wagons. They also manufacture the famous Rocky Mountain freight wagon, the Leadville quartz wagon, and a line of ponderous timber wagons, employed in the construction of the Atchison, Topeka & Santa Fe road. They also manufacture a full line of spring wagons to order.

The company commenced business about six years ago, and now they are manufacturing 7,000 wagons per annum, and employ a capital of half a million of dollars. In their wood material they carry a supply sufficient for four years. So that no material of that kind goes into the hands of the workmen until it has been thoroughly seasoned from three to five years. The reader can form something like an adequate idea of this mammoth establishment when we state that they turn out thirty wagons per day, or one wagon every twenty-five minutes. They get their supply of hubs from Wisconsin, felly and spokes from Indiana, Ohio and other points, and tongues, hounds and lumber for boxes from Ohio, Indiana and Michigan. This lumber is all carefully inspected before being subjected to the seasoning process, and is again inspected before entering the workshop. In another part of this work will be found an engraving of their factory, which is situated about five miles south of the City, on the line of the Missouri Pacific railway. The building to the right, as shown in the engraving, a solid three-story brick structure, 50x600 feet, is employed in the making of wood works and painting, while the building to the left, a one-story brick, 50x300 feet, is where the wagons are ironed. The commodious dry-houses and sheds for the storage of manufactured wagons and stocks are not shown in the engraving, although at the time the writer visited the establishment in April last, they formed a very interesting feature in the works. The machinery employed is of the most perfect description, some considerable portion having been invented by J. P. Gamble, Esq., superintendent of the establishment. This machinery in the hands of skilled workmen, who are under the immediate eye of an experienced foreman, performs the work without a single mistake. Then again, every part of the work is thoroughly inspected before going to the painting department. So that every wagon that goes from their works is as perfect as the best of material and human skill can make it. And it is owing to this system of care and watchfulness that the Kansas wagon is indebted for its wide-spread popularity,

The company employ 253 men; 93 in their blacksmithing department; 36 in the gearing; 22 in the body shops; 23 in the painting departments and 29 in the yards.

The motive power employed is a 250-horse power engine, put up this season. Having thus briefly glanced at the physical features of this immense establishment, let us for a moment contemplate the mental forces that shape and control it, as brains is certainly the substructure upon which money, muscle and machinery has been enabled to build this great manufacturing enterprise. The president of the company, and one of its founders, is the Hon. A. Caldwell, who came to Kansas at an early day and engaged in overland freight-ing to the Pacific, a business in which he was eminently successful. Previous to coming to this State he was engaged in the banking business at Columbia, Pa. Without ever seeking public position, or taking any active part in political matters, he was in 1870 elected United States Senator from this State, and it was mainly to his effort, while a member of that body, that Leavenworth is indebted for the locating and building here by the Government of the military prison; also for the locating here of the United States Court.

about the only favors that have ever been secured to the city from the Government. It was also through his immediate effort, influence and money, that the Missouri River railway was built from this place to Kansas City, and subsequently extended to Atchison, the only line of road that ever lived up to its agreement with the people of this city. He is now the president of the St. Louis & Northwestern road. Such is a brief outline of the breadth of character of its president.

C. B. Brace, treasurer of the company, has been a citizen of Leavenworth for over twenty-four years. Previous to becoming a member of this company, he was for many years engaged in the wholesale hardware business. He is a gentleman of fine business qualifications, and like his associates, takes a lively interest in the development of the City and State. In response to the question as to his opinion on the future of the City and State, he said: "With its rich soil and admirable climate, Kansas must become one of the leading agricultural States of the Union. And, looking at Leavenworth with an impartial eye, I think it an excellent city for both mercantile and manufacturing and I can see no reason why it should not become the most important market center on the Missouri River. The fact of its being a military post is worth hundreds of thousands of dollars to the city annually, as through it a large number of military posts to the West are supplied."

The secretary's desk is occupied by J. B. McAfee, who has been a citizen of the State since 1855. He is widely and favorably known throughout the West. He has filled several positions of honor and trust since his residence here, among which were Secretary of State and Adjutant-General. He is a gentleman of quick perceptions and broad views, both commercially and politically.

J. P. Gamble, superintendent of the company, is a practical wagonmaker of large experience, having been many years in the business at Cairo, Illinois, previous to locating here. C. Townsend, Esq., the General Agent of the company, is an accomplished gentleman, full of energy and ability, and one of the most efficient of wagon men; and so we might speak of many others of this progressive company, but space will not permit. The business office of the company is on Delaware street, and if the reader should ever find himself in Leavenworth, with a few hours leasure, he could not spend it to better advantage than in visiting the Kansas Wagon Works.

In conclusion we will say to such as contemplate moving to this State that it will be to their advantage not to bring their heavy goods, such as farm implements and furniture as they can buy all such here as cheap or cheaper than at the East.

COAL.

THE LEAVENWORTH COAL COMPANY

was organized in 1863, with a capital of $100,000. But little was done towards developing the interest however, until 1868, when a re-organization of the company was affected, the capital increased to $300,000 and the work of opening one of the most valuable and extensive coal mines west of Ohio was pushed forward with such rapidity that the coal of the company was placed on the market in the fall of 1870. The management of the company consists of Lucian Scott, president; Matthew Ryan, vice-president; Lyman Scott, treasurer, and Dr. T. Sinks, secretary, all gentlemen of business push and enterprise, who have been citizens of this city since 1856. That they have succeeded in developing the industry to an extent that has already proved of incalculable value to the City and State is evidenced by the fact that they are now employing 220 men during the summer months, 300 during the other seasons, and are mining on an average 300 tons of coal per day, for which they find a ready market at home and throughout the West. This coal contains, as shown by chemical analysis, 56 per cent. carbon, while the best bituminous coal of Pennsylvania only contains 64 per cent. In fact, it is pronounced by railways and manufacturers as far superior to any other Western coal for steam making. The company are sinking a second shaft, which will be completed about the 1st of July next, which will double their capacity. They have bored an additional depth of 300 feet, striking a vein of a different quality, which will be opened up next year.

Without going into details we will say that the coal mines of Leavenworth are inexhaustible; the quality far superior to other Western coal, and that it is, and will continue to be, the basis of a prosperous manufacturing city and a source of wealth to the whole State

FURNITURE.

ABERNATHY, DOUGHTY & HALL.—SUCCESSORS TO ABERNATHY BROS.

The subjoined engraving is a very cramped representation of the extensive wholesale and retail furniture house of Abernathy Brothers, established in 1860, and located on Delaware street, between Third and Fourth streets. It is a three story and basement brick structure, 50x100 feet, plain in its exterior, but on entering it one finds himself lost in a wilderness, as it were, of elaborate and richly fashioned furniture. The ground floor is divided into two compartments, one being devoted to the handling of carpets, curtains, cornices, lambrequins, etc., embracing the products of both this country and Europe. Here one can select anything desired, from the common hemp to the richest velvet. The other half of the floor is used for office purposes and sales and sample room for the different styles of escritoires, book cases, sideboards, wardrobes, bureaus, dressers, easy chairs, etc., all of beautiful designs and the most elaborately carved. The second floor is used as a salesroom for parlor and chamber sets, of every conceivable style and description. Some of the parlor sets are upholstered in silk, velvet or plush, while others are dressed in the more modest rep, damask or haircloth. Here one can select for a cottage or palace, and that too—for the simple reason the goods are manufactured here—at lower prices than would have to be paid for the same class of goods in St. Louis or Chicago. And, by way of parenthesis, the writer for the benefit of such as contemplate moving in this direction from the East, will say: do not freight heavy goods, such as furniture and agricultural implements, as you can buy here as cheap, and in many instances cheaper than at the East. The third floor is used for the more common grades of furniture, chairs, etc., while the basement is employed for storage and packing. Connected and owned by this house is the most extensive furniture factory in the West. To fully appreciate the extent and magnificence of the furniture handled by the house one must visit it. As an index, however, we will say that the firm employs 100 men and transact an average annual business of $225,000. Their goods are distributed generally through the West, the retail houses in different directions buying largely. J. L. Abernathy, to whose liberal business enterprise the city is indebted for this large and valuable industry, located here in 1853, being one of the very first settlers, and he has always made the advancement of the city's interest identical with his own. In speaking of the present and future of Leavenworth he said to the writer: "Indications point unmistakably to the fact that Leavenworth will continue to grow as a manufacturing city. There are more goods manufactured here now than in all of the other cities in the State. What we particularly want here is more capital in manufacturing and a larger buying market for agricultural products. In short, it offers superior manufacturing advantages, while in the wholesale mercantile line all that is needed are stocks to compete with other market centers. As a whole, the prospects are better than they have ever been before."

Mr. Doughty, a partner in the establishment, has been with the house for eight years, while Mr. Hall has been with it five years. They are gentlemen of sterling worth and enterprise. There is one thing deserving of mention, they manufacture all their own goods. They have a wholesale house on the corner Main and Choctaw streets 50x150 and four stories in height.

ROBERT KEITH & CO.

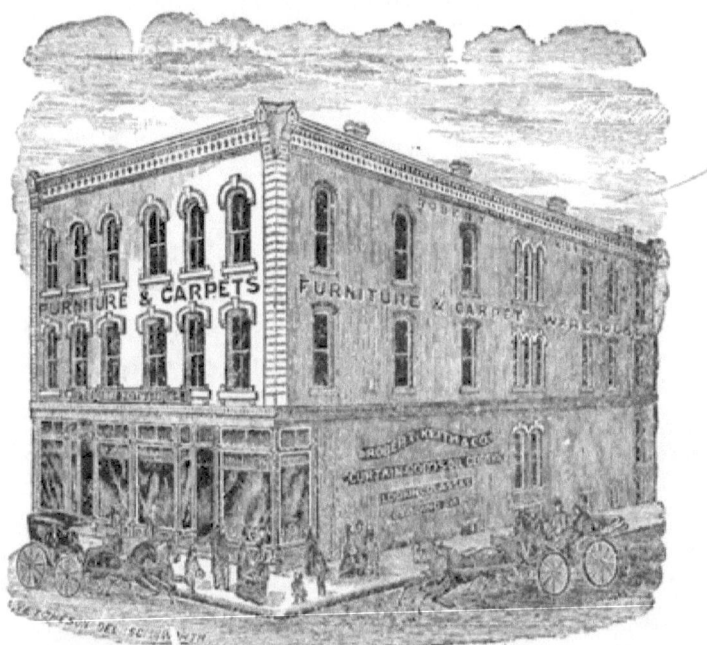

The above cut is an outside view of the furniture house of Robert Keith & Co., and the following, clipped from the Leavenworth *Times*, gives the outside world an idea of what this mammoth establishment are doing:

"ANOTHER MOVE IN THE RIGHT DIRECTION."

"Since the firm of Robert Keith & Co. was established in 1873, it appears that every important business move made by them has been wise and judicious. In 1873 they were doing a retail business at 207 Delaware street. Desirous of increasing their retail trade, the carpet and curtain branches were added, which proved successful. In 1875 it was thought best to combine wholesale with their retail furniture and carpet business. In order to do this successfully it was necessary to make arrangements for the manufacturing of their goods, which they did with the old reliable furniture factory of Dillworth & Lysle, on Cherokee street. Then it was that the business of Keith & Co. began to assume large proportions and it became a necessity to move into larger quarters. The mammoth store, corner of Third and Delaware, was erected and occupied by Keith & Co., in January, 1877, which is used for their retail department, while their wholesale department is carried on in the immense ouilding, corner of Main and Delaware streets. The marked success of this worthy firm has been the subject of much comment throughout the West. Their business has increased greatly year by year, and stands to-day as one of the leading commercial houses on the Missouri river. Mr Robert Keith has been the active manager of this establishment, and has been directed in all important moves by the liberal policy and good business sense of Mr. Levi Wilson, the senior member of the firm. The new accessions of Mr. Wm. Parmlee and Mr. Jos. Keith to the firm will add greatly to its strength, and is another move in the right direction, for both of the new members are known to be men of sterling worth, and first class business capacity. The encouragement which Mr. Wilson offers to these young men to build up such an establishment is certainly very creditable and is appreciated by the community."

MEDICINES.

Among the more useful and rapidly expanding manufacturing enterprises of Leavenworth is the

BROWN MEDICINE AND MANUFACTURING COMPANY.

organized with a capital of $50,000, in August, 1876. The company is composed of enterprising, experienced gentlemen, its officers being Geo. A. Eddy, president; W. C. McPike, vice-president; R. J. Brown, superintendent and treasurer and J. P. Bauserman, secretary. The company have twenty-two persons in their employ and five traveling salesmen; their goods are generally distributed throughout all the Western States and Territories; their sales increasing at the rate of thirty per cent. a year. In the first place this company manufacture a line of medicines especially adapted to the various diseases incident to the Western States and Territories. These medicines are compounded by the most experienced chemists—graduates from the best known schools of pharmacy at the East—under the immediate supervision of Dr. R. J. Brown, an experienced pharmaceutical chemist of long standing who has made the remedies of this company a study for the past twenty years, and that these medicines are filling a want not heretofore met by Eastern remedies, their popularity amply verify And it is a fact worthy of note that none but drugs of ascertained purity enter into their compounds. Besides a full line of medicines, including Brown's Liver Pills, Blackberry and Ginger, Cough Balsams, Tar Troches, Extracts of Jamaica Ginger, Sarsaparilla and Dandelion; they manufacture a large line of popular flavoring extracts, perfumeries, soda syrups, medicated wines, etc. But what is of great importance, all of their galenical and pharmaceutical preparations, also their elixirs, fluid extracts and medicinal syrups are manufactured by experienced chemists from pure materials. Theirs are no patent nostrums, and their business is no experiment, having outlived that hour by developing into the most complete success.

A few words relating to their system of doing business may prove of interest and in a measure account for their large sales throughout the West. In no instance are their goods handled on commission, they are sold direct to the trade on the following conditions: The stock of the company is divided into shares of $50 each, and the druggist who buys $50 worth of these medicines is credited on the company's books with $5 paid on the stock, and when his purchases reach $500 he will have a credit of $50, which he may take in stock or in medicines. This is a most admirable system, as it makes druggists directly interested in promoting the sales of these valuable medicines. The company's books show that there are over 3,000 druggists in different portions of the West that are handling these medicines on the above plan, and as the real value of the system becomes more thoroughly understood, it will become generally adopted and the scope of usefulness of these medicines will be largely increased. The office salesroom and laboratory of the company are situated on Delaware street, and are commodious and most admirably arranged, the laboratory being supplied with all of the most approved appliances for a scientific and successful preparation of these compounds.

R. H. T. NESBITT,

Chemist and Druggist, is located at the corner of Fifth and Miami streets, where he established his present business in 1878. He came here from Montreal in 1872, having graduated at the Montreal Pharmaceutical College in that city. He had fourteen years experience in the drug business before locating for himself. He makes a specialty of preparing prescriptions, and his store was furnished inside under his own direction, and is one of the best fitted in the West. He carries a full line of all the leading drugs, and, in fact, everything usually kept in a first-class drug store

THE LEAVENWORTH SUGAR COMPANY.

A VALUABLE INDUSTRY TO THE CITY.

The announcement made a few months ago that Leavenworth was to have added to her manufacturing industries a large sugar factory, has been realized, and in the combination of local and Eastern capital, we can point with pride to the largest and most completely equipped Glucose, or corn sugar factory in this country : a factory where 2,000 bushels of corn per day, or 730,000 bushels per annum will be converted into sugar or syrup. The Leavenworth Sugar Company was organized in January, 1880, with a capital of $75,000 Their factory is situated about one mile to the south of the heart of the city, the building employed being a three-story brick, 130x140 feet, the machinery and appliances being of the most approved description, the whole costing about $40,000. They employ, as motive power, three engines—the main one being a 150-horse power machine. The establishment furnishes employment for one hundred persons. The management of the Company consists of Lucien Hawley, of Buffalo, New York, a gentleman of large means and broad business views. J. W. Dever, who was for several years the owner of a sugar factory in Cuba, General Superintendent, and Nicholas A. Jones, formerly a prominent contractor on the New York and Erie Railroad, Chief Engineer. In short, the company possess ample capital and the most thorough knowledge of the business, hence with them it is no experiment. The products of the company will be confined to table syrup, sugar and Glucose.

The average yield is about twenty-eight pounds of sugar to the bushel of corn, or twenty-five pounds of syrup. The offal from 2,000 bushels of corn is ample food for 1,500 head of cattle, and is pronounced as far superior to still slops.

There are several establishments of this kind in operation in this country, and as a rule, they are all doing a good business, and the one here, under its present able management, gives promise of being equally prosperous. One thing is certain, and that is, it is one of the most valuable and important industries in the City or State. The industry will not only open a market for nearly a million bushels of corn annually, but will furnish employment for an immense volume of labor. Then, again, for stock feeding, it will prove of great value to both City and State. Hence as a whole, Leavenworth is lucky in securing the location here of the industry, and the company are happy over the promising future of their great enterprise.

M. G. POST,

manufacturer and dealer in harness and saddlery, came to this city, from Illinois in 1879. He has had ten years experience in the business, and has the reputation of turning out as good work as can be found anywhere — East or West. His sales for last year were $3,000.

THE MANUFACTORIES OF LEAVENWORTH.

As the wealth and prosperity of communities, States and Nations are largely dependent on their manufacturing resources, for the information of the many thousands in the Eastern States and Europe to whom this work will be sent, we have devoted a chapter—which will be found in another part of this book—to the present and prospective developments of manufacturing in this city and the many advantages it offers to all who are looking in this direction for business locations. Having laid the whole matter before the reader in a plain, straightforward manner, without indulging in any rose-tinted statements, in the chapter referred to, as an evidence of the important position Leavenworth has reached as a great manufacturing center; it is now proposed to devote a chapter to the more prominent manufacturing industries in prosperous operation at the present time. Giving the largest and most valuable to the City and State the preference, we will first call the attention of the reader to the

GREAT WESTERN MANUFACTURING COMPANY,

established in 1858, the oldest and by far the largest establishment of the kind west of the Mississippi River. Its products include stationary and portable engines of any and all descriptions and of any capacity ordered, saw mills, shafting, pulleys, mill gearing of all descriptions, pumps, mining machinery, horse powers, iron building work, iron fencing, water wheels, bridge bolts, etc. They also handle to a large extent portable flour mills, smut and separating machines, bolting cloth, rubber and leather beltings, mill stones and mill furnishing goods of every description.

Their works cover about ten city lots, each 50x250 feet, or a total of 625 feet square. Their buildings are solid brick structures of attractive exterior, while interiorly they are provided with the most approved machinery and other appliances for manufacturing superior work on a large scale. Their buildings and machinery cost over $75,000, and they do an average annual business of $175,000. They employ 150 persons and keep three traveling salesmen on the road their products being distributed pretty generally through Kansas, Missouri, Colorado, Nebraska and Southern Iowa. They melt about ten tons of iron each day, using Missouri, Tennesse and Scotch pig.

Such is a brief view of this great manufactory, so valuable to the city. Now let us indulge in a glance at the management, at the brain force, that has controlled and developed the enterprise. E. P. Wilson is president, John Wilson, treasurer, and D. F. Fairchild, secretary, all three being among the first settlers of the city, and we only echo the general voice in the statement that none have contributed more towards building up Leavenworth than the gentlemen just mentioned. They are gentlemen of broad business views, large enterprise and highly esteemed in business circles. It may not be out of place to state in this connection that Mr. John Wilson has filled several public positions of honor and trust, including that of State Senator, being at the present time President of the Board of Education.

In 1866 this company commenced to manufacture stoves, and that branch of their business so increased as to necessitate in 1875, the organization of the

GREAT WESTERN STOVE COMPANY.

of which John Wilson is president, E. P. Wilson, treasurer and N. H. Burt, secretary. Although the Great Western Manufacturing Company and the Great Western Stove Company are operated under different firm names, their interests are in a great measure identical. As in the case of the first mentioned company, this is also the most extensive manufacturing enterprise of the kind in the West, and what is more to the point, in quantity, variety and quality they rank second to no stove works in the country. At the present time they turn out about ninety different styles and varieties of cooking and heating stoves, with arrangements for introducing a dozen or more new styles this season. Their stoves have earned such a reputation throughout the West that it is difficult for the company to keep even pace with their orders. They melt about fifteen tons of iron per day, or 4,685 tons a year, and turn out about 25,000 stoves per annum, their trade having increased fully thirty-five per cent. during the past year, their main field of distribution being Kansas, Missouri, Colorado and Nebraska. They employ 125 men, and keep three traveling salesmen on the road.

Thus it will be seen that these two companies, operated on the same premises, and mainly by the same members, employ in the aggregate 275 persons, and have invested in buildings and machinery fully $150,000, while their joint products will not vary much from $350,000 per annum. It is an enterprise of the "manner born," and not only Leavenworth but the whole State is proud of it.

THE SOAP FACTORY OF R. B. CRAIG.

the oldest in the State of Kansas; was established in this city in 1857, and is now one of the valuable industries of Leavenworth. The products of the establishment includes the "Water Lily," "Woman's Friend," "White Russian," "Indigo Blue," "Extra Family," "Olive," "Continental," "Palm" and "Toilet" soaps. These soaps find a ready market throughout Kansas, western Missouri and Colorado; and as their quality is equal to the products of any factories at the East, the business, which now averages $20,000 a year, is steadily increasing. Mr. Craig was formerly in the business at Pittsburg, Pennsylvania, and fully understands how to make soaps that will gain the public favor. He employs seven men in his factory and one on the road.

THE KANSAS CORSET.

Among the numerous manufactures of Leavenworth, "The Kansas Corset," made by Mrs. L. D. Taylor, is receiving considerable attention. What she claims for them over the common corset is perfect fitting, fine finish and durability, which imparts symmetry of form, and the fine quality of material used. She makes both the short and the abdominal corset. She has lately opened in new quarters, at 205 Fourth street, the front room of the store being used as a salesroom for millinery and ladies' neck ware. Mrs. Taylor makes a specialty of corsets to order, and persons in the country adjoining Leavenworth will receive circulars giving full description and prices by addressing her.

THE FLOURING MILLS OF LEAVENWORTH.

THE LARGEST IN THE WEST.

The writer has visited many of the more prominent cities in this country, and while examining the different industries has inspected a large number of flouring mills, and without the least desire to flatter the people of Leavenworth, or to inflict a puff on Mr. H. D. Rush, proprietor of the Leavenworth Mill, we can say that we have inspected no mills East or West that were better arranged or that were better supplied with approved machinery and other modern appliances for facilitating the manufacturing of a superior article of flour than his. And right here we will state that, notwithstanding Kansas City indulges in the penchant of elevating her nasal organ when comparing her commerce with that of Leavenworth, there is more flour manufactured by the Leavenworth Mill alone, than at all of the flouring mills of Kansas City. This is a pretty broad statement, and yet it is just as true as it is broad. To the more distant readers of this work a brief description of this mill may prove interesting. It is a four story and basement brick, 95x100 feet, painted a dark drab, and is situated on the southeast corner of Broadway and Delaware street. It is supplied with eight run of stone and has a capacity of 1,500 bushels per day (12 hours), and is kept running day and night, so pressing is, and has been the demand for its products for the past two years. That a superior quality of flour is produced, it is only necessary to say that it readily commands 25 cents per sack in the market more than any other flour manufactured in the country. The machinery employed is of the most approved description and so thoroughly do the different cleaning and purifying machines do their work, the wheat before passing into the hoppers over the stones is entirely cleaned of all smut, dust or other impurities. And it may be well to give a detailed statement of the various cleansing processes to which the grain is subjected before being reduced to flour. The grain is received into a large hopper placed on an iron track at the front of the building near the east side; this track extends from the entrance at that point to scales employed in weighing the grain. This hopper is rolled out on the platform, filled with wheat from the wagon of the seller and then rolled back on the scales, where the grain is weighed, after which it passes from the hopper into a large receiving bin on the floor below, when the hopper is again rolled to the entrance and refilled and the work of receiving goes on in an easy manner. From the receiving bin, by the aid of elevators, the grain is conveyed to the fourth story, where it is subjected to the first cleansing process by passing through large and excellently arranged warehouse seperators, and from thence to the grading bins, after which it is again introduced into a large Moline separator. It is then subjected to the scouring process, the machine used in this department being manufactured by Hughs & Co., of Hamilton, Ohio. The grain then passes through a fine brush machine, also manufactured by Messrs. Hughs & Co. This last machine effectually removes all dust and other matter from the surface of the grain. Leaving the brush machine the grain passes through a large rolling screen, supplied with a powerful air blast, which removes any and all remaining dust. Then comes the last and finishing preparatory process, from the rolling screen it passes into a combined steamer and dryer, an improved process for toughening the bran. It is then elevated into tight bins, where it remains until manufactured into flour. After being ground into flour, the flour is elevated to the fourth floor where it passes through some nineteen bolting reels and four improved purifiers, which thoroughly separates the pure flour from bran and other matter. The flour then passes through two large Eureka packers to the first floor, where it is sacked and ready for the market. To drive the machinery of this mammoth establishment a 140-horse power engine is employed, the steam being generated by a battery of three boilers, each eighteen feet long, with thirty-two flues. Two powerful steam pumps are used for feeding water, the water being drawn from the Missouri River by independent water works built by Mr. Rush. The machinery employed to drive the stones is of the most improved description and is so adjusted that there is a marked absence of that noise and jar so usual in flouring mills. In fact, Mr. Rush has allowed no expense to interfere in making his mill as perfect as money and human skill could accomplish, and as a reward, he sees his celebrated " Premium " and " Golden Eagle " brands standing at the head of the flour manufacturing industry of this country; and, notwithstanding the immense capacity of his mill, he cannot keep even pace with the constantly increasing demand. This mill is comparatively fire proof, one prevention against conflagration being a brick smoke stack 75 feet in height. Mr. Rush buys only the best winter wheat, of which he carries an average stock of from 75,000 to 125,000 bushels. The flour from this mill is distributed throughout the West, Kansas, Missouri, Iowa, Illinois, Nebraska, Colorado, Texas, New Mexico and the Indian Territory.

About thirty feet west of the above mill, as will be seen by the engraving accompanying this article, is a fine elevator now under process of constructionby Mr. Rush. It fronts 80 feet on Delaware street, is 124 deep, 56 feet in height, with a capacity of 180,000 bushels of grain. When this elevator is completed the grain will enter it from wagons and will move onward, passing through the various processes for cleansing, seperating and purifying never stopping in its forward movement until reduced to flour and sacked for the market. In conclusion we will say, if by choice or chance the reader ever visits Leavenworth and is anyways interested in flour making, he or she, as the case may be, cannot spend an hour more pleasantly than by calling at the Leavenworth Mills. In developing the flour manufacturing interest to its present proportions Mr. Rush has added materially towards building up and infusing life to the various industries of the city.

THE KEYSTONE MILLS.

Of which J. R. Dillworth and J. C. Lysle are proprietors, was built some ten or twelve years ago, and up to 1875 was used as a corn mill. It has three run of stone, is supplied with all approved machinery for making a superior flour and has an easy capacity of 125 barrels per day. Its special brands are the "Golden Sheaf" and "White Swan," which has a reputation equal to any flour made in the West, the demand for which is such that this mill is run to its fullest capacity to meet the shipments to Missouri, Iowa and Illinois.

Adjoining their mill Messrs. Dillworth & Lysle have a large furniture factory, in which they employ twenty-five men, their annual trade in that line being about $25,000. As specialties they manufacture chamber sets, drawer work, desks and tables, which they wholesale throughout the West. Messrs. D. & L. are enterprising men, and their trade shows a healthy expansion. They said to the writer: "After ten years' actual business experience here we do not hesitate in the opinion that the future of Leavenworth is most promising. We have elements of success in manufacturing offered by no other town in the West, and in our opinion it is and will be to Kansas what Lowell is to Massachusetts.

Another of the valuable industries of Leavenworth is the carriage factory of

S. L. NORTH & CO.,

established in 1863, which employs fifty-two skilled workmen, clerks, etc., and we only echo the general voice when we say that their carriages, for style and quality, are equal to any manufactured in this country. They make on an average twenty-five carriages and buggies a month, which find a ready market in Kansas, Missouri, Colorado, Nebraska, New Mexico and Texas. Their factory is 50x300 feet, and in its machinery and other appliances for producing superior work it is the most admirably equipped establishment in the West. Only second growth hickory is used, while all timber employed is most thoroughly seasoned. They make a general assortment of light carriages, buggies, phaetons and trotting sulkies, all of which are kept in stock or made to order, the sales of the company average $60,000 a year, and their trade is increasing. Admirers of fine carriages visiting our city should take the opportunity of looking through the repository of this company.

THE BUCKEYE CARRIAGE WORKS—JOHN CRETORS.

now located on Cherokee street, are the outgrowth of a business established in 1865. Mr. Cretors makes a specialty of the finest class of carriage work. The factory is now crowded to its utmost capacity in filling present contracts for a number of elegant phaetons, fine buggies, spring trucks, furniture vans, etc., besides a large number of spring wagons of various styles. He has at present a working force of twenty men, distributed in the various departments. His business this year will approximate $50,000. Mr. Cretors is an active business man and has been engaged in the carriage making and painting since 1838, and his constantly increasing business is mainly due to the personal supervision, which, from his long experience, he is able to give to the various departments, indicating the popular and growing reputation of this establishment for satisfactory and first-class work.

Among the carriage manufacturers worthy of notice we call attention to

J. LYON,

who unfurled his business banner to the breeze here in 1875, is a solid two-story brick, 50x75 feet, situated at No. 314 and 316 Shawnee street. Mr. Lyon is a pleasant, thorough-going business gentleman, and his work is not excelled by that of any factory in the West. None but proficient workmen are employed, and as all work passes under his immediate supervision, nothing but first-class carriages are allowed to go out from his place. Said Mr. Lyon to the writer: "I do not attempt to compete with the shoddy work made at some points East and sent West for sale: yet I do compete, and will place my buggies and carriages against those of the best factories of the country, East or West. I employ the best material to be had, and I turn out honest, perfect work, a system that has secured me a trade of over $6,000 a year—a trade that is increasing at the rate of 25 per cent. There are some, it is true, that will invest in cheap Eastern work; but they seldom repeat the experiment." Mr. Lyon employs seven men, and carries an average stock of $3,000 in fine buggies and carriages.

THE LEAVENWORTH WOOLEN MILLS,

of which Owen Duffy is proprietor, have been in operation since 1871, and having outlived the days of panics and shrinkages in values, are to-day classed as one of the prosperous industries of the city. It is what is known as a "Three-set Mill," and its products include the different grades of cloths — from the more common tweeds to choice beavers and doeskins. It uses; on an average, 150,000 lbs. of wool, per annum—its products being from $60,000 to $65,000. It furnishes employment for forty persons and is well provided with improved machinery, which is driven by a fine fifty-horse power engine. Mr. Duffy has been a citizen of this city since 1857, and even in the darkest days of its business history, he has never lost confidence in its ultimate success.

AGRICULTURAL IMPLEMENTS.

LEWIS MAYO,

who combines the business of farm machinery, agricultural implements, farm and garden seeds, and groceries, and whose place of business is Nos. 223, 225 and 227 Shawnee street, his store being a two-story basement brick, 50x125 feet; he commenced business in this city in 1866. He employs eight men in his store and one traveling salesmen, and does an average business of $75,000 a year. We have not the space to enter into the details of his stock further than to say, he carries a full line of staple and fancy groceries, which he sells at wholesale and retail, a complete assortment of seeds, with a large variety of farm implements and tools. In farm machinery he handles the most popular makes, making a specialty of N. C. Thompson's celebrated sulky plows and I. X. L. stirring plows, the John Deere plows and cultivators, the Walter A. Wood harvester and self-binder, the Marsh harvester, Empire and Excelsior reapers and mowers, Heebner & Son's Little Giant Threshers, etc. He is general Western agent for the Bellville separator, Harrison wagon and I. X. L. grain drill. He was also appointed recently, Western agent for the Walter A. Wood twine binding harvester, said to be the most economical and successful binder yet invented. He is also agent for the Kansas wagon. Mr. Mayo has drawn in this direction an enormous trade, not only for farm machinery but for groceries. Having thus briefly referred to the business of this house, for the benefit of the more distant readers of this work, we will quote his own words in relation to Leavenworth: "Speaking from my own experience, I believe there is no better point in the West than this for the distribution of agricultural goods, and, notwithstanding Kansas City got the railroads, in my opinion, this will develope into a great manufacturing center. The abundance of cheap coal at our very doors is securing and must continue to secure to us that important industry. The general stagnation in business incident to the shrinkage in values during the past decade, together with local causes, somewhat checked the prosperity of Leavenworth, but those obstacles have been outlived, and with a return of confidence there is a corresponding return of prosperity. With the most liberal religious and school advantages and a healthy climate there is no more inviting city in the West for residence purposes."

Mr. Mayo took an active part in the late war, and at its close entered the Treasury Department at Washington, where he remained until he came to this city.

W. DAVIS,

general dealer in farm machinery, agricultural implements, seeds, sewer pipe, grind stones, etc., has been in the business in this city for the past fourteen years, his sales in 1879 being about $65,000, or about $10,000 larger than in 1878. And he seems sanguine that for the present year, taking the past three months as a criterion, that his sales will reach $100,000. He handles the most popular makes of plows, cultivators, seeders, reapers and mowers, farm wagons and thrashing machines, and, in fact, a large and complete line of everything in the way of farm and garden implements and seeds. His trade, although largely of a local character, extends to a considerable extent into Missouri, Colorado and Nebraska, and is reaching out further and further every year. He also handles the Studebaker and Milburn wagons.

THE UNION MACHINE WORKS,

is another of the important manufacturing industries of this city, that is deserving of especial mention in this work. These works were established in May, 1879, with a capital of $50,000 ; they give employment to about sixty men, and keep one traveling salesman on the road. Their products include a full line of the different varieties of wood and coal stoves, iron fronts for buildings, all kinds of machinery, engines to order, etc. Their specialties, however, are stoves and building iron, in which lines they are doing a large business. Joseph Whittaker, who, previous to his locating here, some twelve years ago, was a prominent pork merchant of Cincinnati, Ohio, is president and treasurer; Moses Harvey, vice-president; A. G. Chandler, secretary, and J. H. Behee, superintendent of the company. They distribute their products throughout the North, West and South—their trade for 1879 being fully one hundred per cent, larger than on the preceding year of the late firm whom they superceded. Their establishment is supplied with the most approved machinery and other appliances for turning out first-class work, and they do a business of about $200,000 per annum. They melt about 4,500 lbs. of iron per day.

THE LEAVENWORTH BAG MANUFACTURING COMPANY,

established in 1874, occupies a prominent position in the manufacturing interests of the city, their trade having increased over 75 per cent, during the past two years, their business now extending throughout Kansas and adjoining States. They occupy four floors in a building, 24x120 feet, work five presses, give employment to thirty persons and keep two traveling salesmen on the road. They manufacture cotton bags, flour sacks and burlaps, and handle a full line paper bags and wrapping paper. W. A. Rose, who has been a citizen of the city for twenty-two years, and who was engaged in the book trade before entering upon his present enterprise, is superintendent and general manager, and in his hands the business has developed into a most complete success.

THE WHOLESALE AND RETAIL JEWELRY HOUSE

OF

R. N. HERSHFIELD.

—

The above engraving is an interior view of the retail department of the great wholesale, retail and manufacturing jewelry house of R. N. Hershfield, the most extensive manufactory of gold and silver jewelry west of New York; and by far the largest wholesale and retail house in this line west of the Mississippi River.

It was established in 1856, and is the oldest house of the kind in the West; while for reputation and business breadth it is the first.

The building occupied is a large and handsome structure, with iron and plate glass front, and is divided into two stores — the first being 25x50 feet, and the second, 25x85 — connected by a large archway at the rear. The main floor of the first, is what we illustrate above, and is used as a retail salesroom. Above this, is the factory, while the basement is used as a storeroom for large and bulky stock — such as watchmakers' and jewelers' lathes, rolls and other machinery, (for which this is the great depot of the West) — as well as for the unbroken packages and cases of silver plated ware, this being the Great Western Agency for all the great manufacturers of these goods in New England.

The main floor of the second store is the wholesale salesroom and offices, and contains five large fire-proof safes — fitted with drawers to hold the smaller and more valuable articles, such as jewelry, watches, chains, diamonds, etc., while the shelves are filled with such goods as watchmakers' and jewelers' small tools and materials, table cutlery, silverware, spectacles and plated jewelry. One side of this room is taken up, almost entirely, with samples of clocks — one each of nearly every style and shape known to the trade; while the room above is devoted exclusively to the storing of the clocks, of which we find here the greatest variety kept by any one house in the country. The basement of this store is the packing room.

It would be an almost endless task to enumerate the different varieties and qualities of goods carried in stock at this establishment — suffice it to say that it handles everything in the line of jewelry; including the products of both America and Europe. In fact, it is the only house west of the Atlantic, where a *full* line of all descriptions of gold and silver jewelry, watches and diamonds, as well as silverware, clocks and materials, can be found under the same roof.

This house employs four traveling salesmen, whose trips extend into almost every county between the Mississippi River and the Pacific, and whose annual sales will reach a quarter of a million. Fourteen skilled workmen are kept busy in the factory, and turn out an immense quantity of the finest goods every year, making to order any design that human imagination can desire.

Mr. Hershfield is a gentleman of broad and liberal views; and during the years of "storm and sunshine" that have passed over Leavenworth, he has ever stood in the foremost rank of those who have aided in developing the City into the great manufacturing center she is to-day.

INSURANCE---FIRE AND LIFE.

Insurance is one of the prominent features in the business of any city, and Messrs. Nelles & Weed, who represent the leading companies of the country, we refer to with pleasure. Their business extends through Kansas, and into Colorado and the Indian Territory. They represent the Home Insurance Company, of New York; Phœnix Insurance Company, of Hartford; Franklin Fire Insurance Company, of Philadelphia; Pennsylvania Fire Insurance Company, of Philadelphia; Springfield Fire and Marine Insurance Company, of Massachusetts, and Imperial and Northern, of London, all of which rank among the first, of first-class insurance companies. The agency was established in 1870, and has been steadily increasing its premium receipts from that time, and has now become the leading agency in the State. They also represent the Mutual Life Insurance Company, of New York, whose assets are larger, surplus greater, premiums lower and dividends higher than those of any other company. The firm consists of George W. Nelles and T. J. Weed, and they are located at the corner of Main and Delaware streets.

WILLIAM T. YOAKUM—Contractor and builder, whose shop is on Delaware, between Fifth and Sixth streets, is an old and esteemed citizen of this city, and is deserving of the liberal patronage he is receiving.

BARBERS' SUPPLIES.

Leavenworth can point to two industries not found elsewhere west of Philadelphia, that of a two-ply carpet mill and a depot where all descriptions of barber goods, either for use or ornamentation, are manufactured and handled at wholesale and retail by

H. J. HELMERS,

at No. 117 Delaware street, where he occupies three floors, 48x80 feet, all of which space he employs as salerooms and for storage and finishing. He has about $15,000 invested in the business, employs twenty-five workmen and one traveling salesman; his trade extending through Kansas, Missouri, Iowa, Nebraska, Colorado and south to the Gulf. Mr. Helmers came to this city in 1859, and has resided here constantly since 1865. He is a gentleman of active business qualifications, and the fact that he has developed the barber supply business into a perfect success is an index to his character. He commenced the selling of this line of goods in 1871, and their manufacture in 1879. Making a specialty of that class of goods his prices range from five to ten per cent. lower than is charged by other firms. This is especially true as relates to chairs, cases, mirrors, and all barber furniture. He keeps in stock all goods used in the barber trade, and has the largest amount of stock on hand of any house in this country. His chairs are the most popular in use.

STEAM BOILERS.

Adjoining the works of the Great Western Machine Company, on Choctaw street, is the

LEAVENWORTH STEAM BOILER WORKS

of Joseph Newsome & Sons, established in 1864. All of the largest and best boilers in use in this city were manufactured at these works. They not only manufacture boilers but make a full line of iron cells for jails also lard rendering and water tanks of all descriptions, and their work has a reputation equal to the best factories East. They make all the boilers sold by the Great Western Manufacturing Company, which is sufficient evidence of their merit. They employ six men and do an average business of $12,000 a year. Mr. N. learned the business in London, England, and has followed it fifty-three years. He came to this country in 1835 and carried on the business seven years in Illinois. They are an enterprising business firm and their work has a high reputation.

The Harrop Grocers' Supply Manufacturing Company.

This enterprise was established in 1876, by Mr. Harrop, who came to Leavenworth in 1868, from Philadelphia. They make a specialty of supplying the trade with pure flavorings, syrups, extracts, oils, etc. The Harrop Baking Powder has a wide reputation for purity among the dealers throughout Kansas and Missouri; as also has his celebrated Dry Hop Yeast, and, in fact, all the articles manufactured by this Company. Mr. Harrop's experience in the manufacture of the above line of goods is a sufficient guarantee that all goods made by him will be just as represented.

BEER MANUFACTURING IN LEAVENWORTH.

There are few people in this city, to say nothing of thousands outside who will read this work, but will be surprised to learn that there are fully 13,000 barrels of beer manufactured here each year, which furnishes a market for nearly or quite 40,000 bushels of barley, and employment for fully fifty persons. This interest alone pays over $13,000 per annum towards the liquidation of the National debt, in the way of revenue tax on its product. There are four breweries in the city which, at a moderate estimate, employ an aggregate capital of $100,000. Without the least desire to advocate temperance or intemperance, we can only say that the beer making industry is a material advantage to the city, and when conducted as it is at the present time, should be encouraged. Of the four breweries in the city, the largest and oldest is that of

MESSRS. BECKER & LINCK,

superior to any other establishment of the kind in the West. Their malt-house, a fine three-story brick, is at 583 and 585 Delaware street, and is a model of the kind, being commodious and airy, and supplied with all conveniences and other appliances for manufacturing a superior quality of malt. Their brewery is situated on Lawrence avenue, about one mile from the heart of the city, and is a large stone building, most admirably adapted to the business. Messrs. Becker & Linck are practical brewers, and under their personal supervision no pains or expense is spared in making their beer a pure, healthful beverage. In fact their "Premium Lager Beer" has a reputation that will not suffer when placed beside the best Milwaukee beer. Besides their large local trade they have a wholesale depot at Emporia, Kansas, to which large shipments are made from week to week. They are also the proprietors of what is known as the Leavenworth Bottling Works, where they do an immense business in the way of bottling ale, beer, soda, selzer waters and ginger ale, which they distribute throughout the West. Messrs. Becker & Linck have not only established a large, prosperous and advantageous trade to the city, but have earned a place among the foremost of Leavenworth's enterprising business men.

In the northern portion of the city is situated the large brewery and bottling works of

MESSRS. BRANDON & KIRMEYER,

where about 5,500 barrels of beer is manufactured ; their capacity being about 300 barrels of beer per week, or 15,000 barrels per annum. This establishment commenced business in 1857, as a soda water factory, and in 1862, commenced the beer-making business. Both members of the firm are old and esteemed citizens. Mr. Brandon having commenced the soda manufacturing trade here in the spring of 1858, while Mr. Kirmeyer commenced the butcher trade in the fall of same year. They make a quality of beer that is popular throughout the West, which, for purity and flavor. compares favorably with the best Milwaukee beer. They use about 12,000 bushels of barley per year, and pay to the Government, in the way of revenue, about $5,500. In connection with their brewery is their bottling works, where they put up ale, beer, soda water and ginger ale — products for which they have a large demand. They employ fourteen men, and command ample capital. In short, they are among the solid, enterprising business men of Leavenworth, and, like their beer, their reputatation stands high.

MARBLE WORKS.

There are two marble works in this city, that of

BURDETT, HEIS & SPOONER,

Manufacturers and wholesale dealers in marble, established in 1862, being the oldest and by far the most extensive. They do all kinds of monumental work, house finishing and furniture marble and building stone, and have recently supplied their works with steam power and machinery for manufacturing furniture tops, in which, as in all other branches, they are prepared to supply the trade at wholesale. They also handle all descriptions of iron fencing for lawns and cemeteries, also a full line of cemetery and lawn furniture. They employ from twelve to twenty-four men and from six to ten traveling men, and do an average trade of $30,000 a year. They carry the largest stock of marble to be found in the West, and they have the reputation of producing as fine work as any house of the kind East or West.

MARBLE AND GRANITE WORK.

We find the above industry well represented in Leavenworth, Mr. Geraughty being the representative of one of the two yards established here. He came here at the close of the war—in which he served—in 1865, and established his present business, and the numerous monuments and tablets that mark the resting place of loved ones in the "city of the dead " in this and adjoining towns are a testimony to his motto that honest work is the best advertisement. His business is on a solid basis, doing about $12,000 a year. He employs six skilled workmen and two salesmen on the road. The yards of the establishment are large, being 125 feet by 50 feet front, and we found in them some superb and artistic pieces of workmanship in the line of monuments, headstones and tablets, etc. In all the localities where Mr. Geraughty's work has had a trial he holds and controls the trade and confidence of his patrons, for he allows no work to leave his yards that is not first-class. Parties wishing any discription of cemetery work will do well to call and examine his stock and they will find that good work and reasonable prices are his motto.

HOTELS.

THE CONTINENTAL HOTEL.

is situated on the corner of Cherokee and Fourth streets, and is the most popular house in the city. It is a three story and basement brick and contains sixty well furnished rooms. As will be seen by the engraving; it fronts both on Cherokee and Fourth streets. The ground floor is devoted to office, dining room, billiard and sample room, reading-room and barber shop purposes. On the second floor are the parlors, reception rooms and a portion of the sleeping apartments, while the third floor is entirely devoted to sleeping apartments. The rooms are clean and inviting and well furnished, commodious sample rooms being provided for commercial travelers. The proprietors, Messrs. Przybylowicz & Fritsche, were among the first settlers in this city, the first came here in 1852, when there was not a single house in the place. He built the Continental in 1868, and Mr. Fritsche became a partner in 1872. No pains are spared to make all who favor this house with their patronage comfortable. It is one of the best $2 per day houses in the West.

THE PLANTERS' HOUSE,

of which J. B. Lambert is proprietor was built in 1856, and is one of the largest hotels west of the Missouri River. It is situated on the corner of Main and Shawnee streets, and from its eastern balcony one has a beautiful view of the river. It contains 100 large, pleasant, well furnished sleeping rooms, finely fitted up parlors and reception rooms, and, in fact, it is provided with all modern improvements for the comfort and convenience of guests. Commercial travelers will find large sample rooms, while pleasure parties will find beautifully furnished rooms, single or en suite, at their disposal. And, what is equally important, they will find Thos. Macken, chief clerk of the establishment, a courteous, genial gentlemen, who never tires in administering to the wants and comfort of guests. Mr. Macken was formerly from Worcester, Mass., and has been in the city only about two years. But without going into details, the Planters is the largest and best hotel in the city. It is to Leavenworth what the Coates' House is to Kansas City.

SOMETHING ABOUT WALL PAPER, GLASS AND PAINTS.

In looking through the above line of business the writer called at the well-known house of

G. P. SCOTT,

on Shawnee street. The business was established in the spring of 1857 by H. P. Scott. Then Leavenworth was in its swaddling clothes and the business was commenced in a small way in a small room, but the business has kept pace with the expansion of the city and now averages fully $6,000 a year, and in place of a small room Mr. Scott now occupies a fine two story stone front, 24x74 feet, and carries a fine stock of wall paper, curtains, glass, paints and varnishes. In fact, he has a full line of decorating and finishing goods, his average stock being about $4,000. He employs ten experienced workmen and during the busy season a larger number. His place is popular with the public and he deservedly enjoys a large and increasing trade.

THE LUMBER INTEREST.

The lumber trade is represented in this city by four yards which carry general stocks, and the following report is made after visiting each yard and a careful investigation of the stock and trade of each. The yard of

J. INGERSOLL,

was established in 1857, and is both the oldest and largest establishment of the kind in the city, and as they do both a local and general shipping trade their business exceeds that of either of the other yards. They carry a general stock, including the different grades of pine, shingle, lath, sash, doors and blinds, mouldings, brackets, etc. They also handle some varieties of hard wood. Messrs. Ingersolls are gentlemen of large experience and broad business views, and having been citizens here since the town was young, as might be expected, they take a lively interest in its development. They said to the writer: "No point in the West offers such advantages for mercantile and manufacturing enterprises as does this city. The abundance and cheapness of fuel alone, to say nothing of the many other advantages, must in the immediate future develope this into the great manufacturing center or the West. All that is needed is active capital and business enterprise."

ROBERT GARRETT & CO.,

is another lumber firm composed of Robert Garrett and Peter Bubb, the former having been in the business ten years and the latter over twenty years. They carry a full line of pine lumber, shingles, lath, sash, doors, blinds, mouldings, etc., also, the different varieties of hard wood, and a stock of the different colors of paints. Their trade for 1879 was about 25 per cent. larger than on preceding year. "It is only a question of time," said Mr. Garrett, "when Leavenworth will become the great manufacturing city of the West; in fact, it is much the largest in the State now — both in population and manufacturing, and as the advantages offered here become more widely known, these industries will increase."

A. J. ANGEL.

has been in the lumber trade here for ten years. He carries a genera stock of pine, oak, ash, hickory and poplar—including the different qualities, also timber, posts, shingles, lath, sash, doors, blinds and paints. His trade is chiefly confined to Leavenworth, Jefferson and Wyandotte counties, in this State, and Platte county on the Missouri side of the river.

SASH, DOORS AND BLINDS.

Among the largest and most widely-known firms engaged in this line of trade is

MUNSON & BURROWS,

whose factory and warehouse are located on Choctaw street, between Fourth and Fifth streets. They commenced business in a small way in 1864, and they now employ forty men, and do an average business of over $100,000 per annum. They are manufacturers of, and dealers in, the different varieties of sash, doors, blinds, stairs, stair railing, balusters, Newell posts, mouldings, etc. They also handle a full line of pine and hardwood lumber. Their trade has had a healthy increase from the start, and is now in a highly prosperous condition. Mr. Munson has been a citizen of this city since 1858, previous to which, he lived in Springfield, Mass. Mr. Burrows was formerly in business in Detroit, Mich., but came to this city in 1864, when the present house was organized and commenced business. Said Mr. Munson : "Some of our business men in years past, became frightened and deserted us, but those who stayed, are to-day, all prosperous."

LEAVENWORTH NOVELTY WORKS.

FOLGER & FAIRBANK,

situated at 114 and 116 Delaware street, established in 1870, and the only works of the kind in the State. They are brass founders and manufacture all kinds of brass goods; they are also model makers, engravers and electroplaters. They employ five men and do a business of over $5,000 per annum. Mr Folger was formerly in business in Detroit, while Mr. Fairbank came here from England. They are both practical workmen, and have the reputation of turning out as good work as any house in the East. In brief, they are skillful workmen and are deserving of the large patronage they are receiving.

GEORGE SMITH

came to this city from Kansas City, some eighteen months since, and established a brass lock factory, for the manufacture of all descriptions of brass and iron locks. It has been a life-long business with him, and as a result, his locks are superior to anything of the kind made in this country. It is a valuable industry to the city, and the public should extend to Mr Smith the patronage that his work deserves.

THE SINGER SEWING MACHINE.

The "Singer" machine is represented by James Farren, who came here in 1857, and has been agent for the "Singer" for twenty years, and has sold 5,000 machines — his annual trade averaging $15,000. He is the oldest sewing machine dealer in the State, and as he handles the old favorite, it is not surprising that he is so successful. He keeps four men on the road constantly. He said : "Prospects for business in this city look brighter than for years. Confidence is being infused into trade ; I have seen the financial cloud come and go in this city, and I now think the hard times are over, and an era of universal prosperity has dawned."

LEAVENWORTH AS A DRY GOODS MARKET.

The dry goods interest in Leavenworth is represented by six large establishments, four of which sell at retail and in job lots, and some five or six smaller establishments—the aggregate sales of all for the year 1879, as far as can be ascertained, were $824,000. A few words descriptive of the different houses engaged in the trade, their age, the extent and character of their business, together with the experience, business breadth of character of their proprietors, with their views on the business of Leavenworth, present and prospective, will undoubtedly prove both interesting and valuable to such as are looking in this direction for business locations or homes. Among the judiciously managed and more prosperous mercantile houses in Leavenworth is the well and favorably known establishment of

GEO. H. WEAVER,

which was founded by Mr. Weaver some five years ago, and its growth from the start has been healthy and substantial. He combines the wholesale and retail branches, to accommodate, which he occupies two floors, 24x125 feet, the first being used for retailing and the second for wholesaling salesrooms. His stock embraces a general line of staple and fancy dry goods, furnishing goods and notions, and his books show a business of $152,000 for 1879, with a marked increase thus far for 1880. Mr. Weaver is one of Leavenworth's oldest citizens, having resided here since 1857, and for the past twenty years he has been prominently identified with the dry goods trade of the city. In 1859 he became connected with the dry goods house of Watson & Rhinehart where he remained until 1865, when he associated himself as junior partner with Fairchilds & Pierce, with whom he continued until 1875, when he established a house of his own. Mr. Weaver is what would be termed a careful, conservative merchant, prompt in his business relations, and most pleasing in his address. He is a most uncompromising advocate of Leavenworth interests, and has always contributed liberally towards its commercial advancement. In speaking of the present and future business of the city, he said: "There is a general revival of business throughout the country, and it has infused a degree of life into trade not witnessed for some time past. In my opinion business prospects here are more promising than at any other time during the past fifteen years. The agricultural interests are in a healthy condition, and taken as a whole, there is a feeling of confidence on every hand, and unless some unforeseen disaster should overtake the city, I feel that we are entering on an era of great prosperity."

Every city has its favorite dry goods houses, where the fashionable do congregate to discuss fashion and colors and to buy the latest styles and novelties, and Leavenworth is no exception, as the dry goods house of

FLESHER & SCHUNEMAN

is to this city what Field, Leiter & Co. is to Chicago, i. e., the popular house. This house was established in 1857, and hence is one of the oldest houses in the State. The firm is composed of B. Flesher and Charles Schuneman, both of whom came to this city at an early day from Europe, their capital consisting chiefly of a thorough business education and upright characters. They occupy a three-story and basement building, 24x115 feet, using the first floor as a retail salesroom and the second floor for wholesaling, while on the third floor is stored their reserve stocks. They carry the largest stock of staple and fancy goods, furnishing goods, novelties and notions of any house in the State, and their annual sales exceed $100,000, and are steadily increasing. Their stock of dress goods and furnishing goods is especially large, and includes everything in the make-up of a lady's toilet, from a hair ribbon to the choicest velvets and silks. Their high reputation secures to them a large trade on mail order account for piece and package goods. Few have done more towards advancing the mercantile growth of Leavenworth than this enterprising firm.

J. H. FOSTER

is one of the leading and prosperous dry goods merchants of this city. He has been a citizen of Leavenworth for fifteen years, the larger portion of the time being prominently identified with the dry goods interest. Previous to his establishing his present business, he was associated in the dry goods trade with the firm of Jaggard & Foster. He occupies a fine store on the southwest corner of Delaware and Fourth streets, fronting twenty-four feet on the former, and one hundred and twenty on the latter thoroughfare. In general terms, he carries a full line of staple and fancy goods, notions and ladies' furnishing goods, including all of the latest novelties in that line. He also handles ladies' ready-made suits, suitings, wraps etc. In brief, his is one of the largest establishments of the kind in the city, also one of the neatest, best arranged and best managed. It is one of the fashionable resorts for ladies for securing fine dresses and dress goods. Mr. Foster's business averages about $75,000 a year, and is increasing. He employs fifteen clerks, and as a rule they are kept busy. Mr. Foster in speaking of the city, said: "It has seen its worst days, and is now improving. I, for one, would not exchange it for Kansas City for my business. I have full confidence in the city."

T. K. FOSTER.

proprietor of the popular dry goods house on Delaware, between Third and Fourth streets, came to this city from Kentucky in 1861, and that he has been eminently successful, his extensive trade, both in the city and country, fully attests. He carries a large stock of staple and fancy goods, notions, etc., making a specialty of ladies' dress goods and furnishing goods. He occupies two floors 24x100 feet, employs eight salesmen, and does a flourishing business. He does both a retail and jobbing trade—his mail order trade having increased largely of late. One feature in his system of business deserves imitation : He turns his goods over rapidly — never burdening his shelves with out-of-date styles. In other words, he keeps fresh goods, adhering to the "nimble sixpence" plan in fixing prices. Mr. Foster is a careful business man, of pleasing address and is held in high esteem by the public.

During our walks and talks among and with the merchants of Leavenworth, a call was made at the well-known dry goods house of

FRANK SCOTT,

formerly in business in Milwaukee, where he was held in high esteem as an enterprising business gentleman. He commenced business here in 1864, and he now has one of the finest stocks of staple and fancy goods, notions and furnishing goods, in the city, and transacts a business of about $85,000 a year. His store is a favorite resort, where ladies congregate to discuss fashions and select the latest styles and novelties in dress and furnishing goods. He employs ten salesmen, hence all customers are waited upon without delay, mistake or confusion. Mr. Scott is a gentleman of quick perception, of easy manners, prompt and reliable in his business relations, and fully understands how to run a dry goods house so as to make it popular with the public. In brief, he is one of Leavenworth's esteemed merchants. He pays special attention to orders from the country at low rates.

MILLINERY AND FANCY GOODS.

Among the more popular places in the city is

WINN'S BAZAAR,

situated at 416 Delaware street, of which T. H. Winn, who was for several years engaged in the dry goods trade at Pekin, Illinois, is proprietor. "The Bazaar" was established in July, 1879, and it has already gained a widespread popularity, and secured a trade of fully $18,000 per annum. Mr. Winn carries a full and complete line of millinery goods, ladies' furnishing goods, and all fancy goods and novelties of the season, with a full line of notions, table linen, gents' furnishing goods, etc. It is a Bazaar in fact, and anything you need in the line of notions, fancy goods, furnishing goods or head gear, you can find there, and as a result, it is a place where ladies "most do congregate" to adorn themselves with the latest styles. His stock is so large, so complete, and embraces such a variety of quality and styles, that it is a common saying, when an article is wanted and cannot be found at other stores, "Go to Winn's and you will get it if it is to be had in the city." They occupy a store 22x85 feet and employ six clerks— all under the immediate supervision of Mr. and Mrs. Winn, both of most pleasing address, and large business experience, and although less than a year here, they have won the confidence and esteem of the public.

If the reader will make a note, as this work is perused, it will be discovered that quite a large per cent. of the solid business men of the city were formerly from the New England States, which, in a measure, accounts for the uniform success that has followed the footprints of mercantile and manufacturing commerce. Among the number hailing from that direction, and who commenced business here eighteen years ago, is the popular firm of

STERN & BROTHER,

who received their business training at Hartford, Connecticut. They are located at 319 and 327 Delaware street, where they occupy two fine stores, 22x100 feet each, from which they distribute millinery, fancy goods and notions, to the extent of $40,000 per annum. They also have a large branch house at Atchison. As an index to their trade it is only necessary to state that they employ fourteen persons in their salesrooms ; while their stock compares favorably with that carried by the larger houses in St. Louis and Chicago. "After a business experience here of eighteen years," said the Messrs. Sterns, "we are entirely satisfied with Leavenworth, both in its present and prospective."

The Commercial Intelligence Office and Kansas Mercantile Agency,

of which Col. E. N. O. Clough is manager and proprietor, stationed at 103 Delaware street, was established in 1872, since which time it has steadily grown in popularity and increased in business, until at the present time it has a revenue of $5,000 per annum. and employs 6,000 local agents throughout the country. And in the statement that it is both reliable and responsible, we only echo the public opinion. Col. Clough has been a resident of Leavenworth for twenty years, and is the head of the oldest house in that business in the West. He came West from Boston in 1833, and has always been intimately identified with Western interests. He went up the Missouri River as far as the headwaters of that stream at a very early date, visiting what is known as the Black Hills. He took a hand in the war with Mexico, serving in a volunteer regiment from Missouri. He also served during the late rebellion, as Colonel of infantry. He is a gentleman of active business habits, pleasing in his address, and has earned the confidence and esteem of the public.

We presume there are but few persons in this city, outside of those directly interested, that comprehend the fact that the house of

STEVENS & GARRIGUES,

general dealers in wagon and carriage hardware, iron, steel, wagon wood work, and hard wood lumber, at 34 Cherokee street, is the most extensive and complete establishment of the kind west of St. Louis. This may seem a bold statement, yet the facts will warrant it. And when we state that their books show an average trade of $140,000 a year, the reader will begin to realize its magnitude. The house was established in 1868 by Mr. Stevens, who was formerly in business at Toledo, where, as here, he was esteemed as an active, enterprising business gentleman. Mr. Garrigues entered the firm in 1874. He, too, is a gentleman of experience, with broad and liberal business views. They employ eleven men in the store and two on the road, and occupy four floors, 50x125 feet, all of which are employed in handling their extensive stock. They carry a full line of hard wood lumber, their yards extending from Cherokee to Choctaw streets. As usual, we asked them their opinion on the future business prospects of the city, to which they responded: "We have an abiding confidence in the continued and increased prosperity of the city. And to prove this, we will say that we investigated the matter carefully, and could see no advantage in locating at Kansas City; hence, we have just moved into, and taken a long lease of this building. This is certainly atar more desirable place to live than in Kansas City, and we are satisfied it offers far better business advantages." They are general western agents for the Eclipse Fan Blower.

THE WHOLESALE LIQUOR TRADE.

This branch of mercantile commerce is represented in Leavenworth by

M. HOFMANN,

the oldest and largest dealer of that class of goods in the State. He has been in business twenty-three years, and hence knows the genuine from spurious or "doctored" stuffs that are handled by those who have less experience in the business. Or, in other words, Mr. Hofmann has earned the reputation of handling honest, pure goods, both of domestic and foreign makes. And in order to accommodate his immense stock, he occupies three floors, 25x100 feet, all of which space he keeps filled with the choicest and most popular brands of wines and liquors. His stock embraces the products of the following popular distilleries, of which he is sole agent: "Hermitage," "Kentucky Club," "Anderson," "W. H. McBroyer," and "Nelson & Wellwood," all of Kentucky, and G. Uckenheimer, of Pennsylvania. He employs seven clerks in his store, and three traveling salesmen, and his trade to-day extends pretty generally through Kansas, Colorado, New Mexico, Nebraska and Missouri, and is still reaching out into the Western Territories. His sales, for 1879, were $225,000, which is not far, if any, below any other wholesale mercantile house in the city. Mr. Hofmann is an active, enterprising gentleman, who has always stood shoulder to shoulder with the leading men of Leavenworth in all enterprises tending to promote the growth and importance of the city. In response to the question as to his views on the present and future outlook for the city he promptly replied, " In my opinion, Leavenworth has reached a bed-rock solidity, and is now building upon a a prosperous mercantile and manufacturing foundation."

BOOTS AND SHOES.

THE WHOLESALE BOOT AND SHOE HOUSE OF CATLIN & KNOX

was established in 1859, and report says, it is the oldest house of the kind in the State. Be that as it may, it has outlived all the disturbing influences that have surrounded commerce for the past twenty years—such as war, panics and depreciation in values—and to-day is doing a good, safe business, their annual sales reaching about $200,000

They are located on Main street, adjoining the Postoffice, where they occupy three floors, 22x110, as sales and storeroom.

They employ three traveling salesmen. They carry a large general stock of all descriptions of Eastern-made boots and shoes, from the more common to the finest and best, but make a specialy of *custom-made* work.

Owning, as they do, their place of business, buying exclusively for cash and being nearer to the consumer, this firm claims advantages over houses located further East, doing perhaps, a lager business, but at an expense which compels larger profits.

To their economy in handling goods, the durability of their work and the fairness in the treatment of their customers, they owe their prosperity and the present rapid increase of their business. They are both enterprising business men, and it is to such that Leavenworth owes her present improved condition. They claim that the general business prospects of Leavenworth have never been as bright as they are to-day.

Among the largest and most popular retail houses of this line of merchandise, is that of

PEMBERTON & CO.,

on Delaware street, between Third and Fourth streets. Their store is 24x125 feet, all available space in which is filled with the best and most popular products of the most widely-known shoe factories of the Eastern and Middle States. In fact, they make a specialty of the best goods manufactured, and their large and growing trade embraces the better class of buyers, both in the city and country. They buy direct from manufacturers, and have several lines of ladies' and gentlemen's shoes — made especially for their trade. In short, they carry a large and complete stock, have a fine store, a prosperous business, and what is equally important to business success, an unblemished reputation, both in commercial and social circles. Their sales range from $40,000 to $45,000 a year, with an average increase of 20 per cent. per annum.

RITCHEY & M'NUTT.

In March, last, Messrs. Ritchey & McNutt established their large boot and shoe house at 313 Delaware street. They have a fine store, tastily arranged, and their stock embraces a full line of ladies', gentlemen's, misses' and childrens' boots and shoes — all new and latest styles — the product of the best factories in the country. They have come to Leavenworth to stay, and they say "if by selling the better class of goods made, at the least money of any house in the city will procure us our share of the public patronage, we shall certainly have it."

All their purchases are made direct from the factories, so that they may buy as low as the largest wholesale house in the country, whereby they can fill orders at wholesale prices.

They pay particular heed to the wants of each customer, who is sure to leave their house well pleased, whether he or she has made a purchase or not.

Among the larger and most popular manufacturers and dealers in boots, shoes and leather, is

FRANK ZIPP,

who owns the fine two-story brick, 24x120 feet, at No. 404 Shawnee street, in which he does business. Mr. Zipp carries one of the best stocks of Eastern-made goods to be found in the West, and also manufactures largely to order. He gives employment to twelve men; carries an average stock of $10,000, and sells about $30,000 worth of goods a year. He is a practical mechanic, and thoroughly understands the boot and shoe trade, hence, no "Cheap John" goods or shoddy work is allowed on his shelves. In other words, he manufactures and deals in the best quality of goods — a system that has secured for him a large and growing trade, and a good reputation throughout the city and country. He is an old citizen and sanguine in the opinion that Leavenworth is destined to become the "Lowell" of the West in manufacturing.

JAMES LANGMORE,

manufacturer and dealer in boots and shoes, has been a resident here since 1856. He occupies a two-story brick, 24x50 feet, employs two men, carries an average stock of $1,500 and does an average business of $3,000. He is an old and esteemed citizen, an experienced workman, and his goods always prove just what he represents them to be. In other words, he is reliable, both as a citizen and business man.

BOOKS, STATIONERY, ETC.

It was Wendell Phillips, we believe, who once said, "the character and society of any town may be fairly measured by the number breadth and character of its book stores." If that be a fact, Leavenworth is a model city, for certainly she has as large and well patronized book houses as can be found in the West. As a measurement of the whole, the writer will speak of the largest and oldest in the city—that of

CREW & BROTHER,

situated on Delaware, between Fourth and Fifth streets, an engraving of which is herewith presented. As will be seen, it is a three-story and basement brick, 24x115 feet. The ground floor is a retail salesroom. Step inside and you will find a large stock of miscellaneous books, blank books, a large line of stationery, wall paper, window shades, curtains and cornices, oil paintings, chromos, steel engravings, picture frames, mouldings, brackets, etc. Ascend the second floor—their wholesale department—and you will find it filled to the ceiling with packages and cases of the goods named before, from which orders from the interior are filled. There you will also find a full line of druggist sundries. The third floor and basement are used for storing duplicate stocks, and packing goods for shipment. Outside of staple works, and a full line of school books, they carry all popular works, periodicals, literary papers, and leading daily prints of the country. They do a large retail trade, while their wholesale business extends through the West—their sales for 1879 being $13,000 larger than in 1878. Their large trade is due to the large variety of goods handled. In fact, it has become a common saying—when one wants an article that cannot be found elsewhere—"Have you been to Crews?" In brief, it is one of the prosperous, solid mercantile houses of the city.

In response to the question as to their views on the present and future of the city, Mr. J. H. Crew said: "Examples are better than any man's opinion. Look at the facts; men who have abandoned Leavenworth have, without scarcely a single exception, failed in business and are, to-day, financial wrecks; while on the other hand, those that remained, are as a rule doing a good business and are prosperous. In this practical illustration you have my full opinion"

At 323 Delaware street, between Third and Fourth streets, is situated the extensive wholesale book and stationery house of

SAMUEL DODSWORTH & CO.

Their stock is large and general, embracing everything in the line of standard books, periodicals, school books, blank books, school supplies, stationery, wall paper, window shades, cornices, curtains, oil paintings, chromos, steel engravings, picture frames, etc. They also carry a full line of paper bags, wrapping and print paper. They occupy three floors and basement, 24x120 feet, employ six salesmen in their store and two on the road, and do a large business, which is constantly increasing. They have had twenty years experience in the business and are well and favorably known. Their trade extends into Colorado, Texas and New Mexico. This is one of the largest houses of the kind west of the Mississippi River, and none in the West is more widely or favorably known. They are also large manufacturers of all kinds of bank and country ledgers and books for such purposes. Their facilities for printing are large and all orders entrusted to them will be filled with promptness.

CLOTHING.

Occupying a fine double store, on the northwest corner of Delaware and **Fourth** streets, 50x100 feet, is the Oak Hall clothing house of

CHAS. M. SALINGER,

who came to this city in 1866. His stock is as large, if not the largest in the city, and includes men and boys' clothing, which he has manufactured expressly for his trade, fine shirts and underwear, which he manufactures, and a fine line of domestic and imported furnishing goods. His system of conducting the clothing trade has earned for him a large trade. In the first place, his garments are fashioned in the latest styles and the material used is of the best, and in the second place, where he retails—for he sells both at wholesale and retail—he allows no garments to go out of his store that do not fit the buyer. Under this system one can select a fashionably cut suit of clothes, made of good material, at from $10 to $20, equal in all respects to custom made. This system has rewarded him with a trade of over $100,000 a year. He said: "Taking my business, as a basis of opinion, Leavenworth is one of the best business cities in the West."

JOHN SECKLER,

proprietor of one of the largest clothing house, located here in 1857 He commenced the clothing trade under the firm name of Seckler & Luhn, in 1863, and to-day his is among the largest establishments in the city, his sales averaging $45,000 per annum. He furnishes employment for ten men, his stock embracing the different varieties of the best clothing made, also a full line of gentlemen's furnishing goods. In 1880 he commenced the merchant tailoring business in company with his son Oscar, that branch of the business being conducted under the firm name of

SECKLER & SON.

They have as fine a stock of American and European made cloths as can be found in the West, and, as Mr. Oscar Seckler learned his trade under one of the best cutters in this country, it is one of the most popular places in the city for elegantly fitting garments. They make a specialty of wedding and party suits, in which line they are having a large trade.

GUENTHER & MACHIN,

men's fine furnishers and manufacturers of "True Fit shirts" at 305 Delaware street, is a firm composed of Will Guenther and Ed. B. Machin, two enterprising gentlemen, who came to this city recently from Chicago, where they had ten years experience in the business. They are practical in their line of trade, have the genuine Chicago business snap, and are carrying a fine stock of underwear and custom shirts. They make a specialty of manufacturing to order, and have already secured a large patronage. They occupy the ground floor and basement, 22x80 feet, the first floor being used as a salesroom, while the basement is fitted up as a laundry, which, by the way, has the reputation of doing as fine work as the best laundries in Chicago, it being conducted on the same system as are the laundries of that city. They are the sole manufacturers of the "True Fit Shirt," which enjoys a high reputation among gentlemen who appreciate a perfect fitting shirt. The young men have made a wise selection in their business location, as their large trade shows.

The Commercial Agency of R. G. Dunn & Co.

was established in this city some eight years ago, and for the past year it has been under the management of S. C. Ashton, who has the reputation of being careful and judicious in the transactions of all ousiness entrusted to him. The business of the agency shows a perceptible increase during the past two years. It has the prestage of being reliable.

CROCKERY, CHINA, GLASS AND SILVERWARE.

Whatever may be said of inadequate stocks, in some channels of the wholesale trade of Leavenworth, and the inability of some of our wholesale houses to keep pace with the growing demand, there is nothing in the way of quantity, variety, quality, or prices that renders St. Louis or Chicago more advantageous markets in which to buy crockery, china, glass and silver-ware than this city. That there is room for improvement in the amount and variety of goods carried by some of the wholesale houses in this city, no one will deny; yet the crockery and glassware trade is an exception, as in these lines ample stocks of the latest and most popular styles are carried. And right here the writer will say that if the wholesale dealers here would only offer equal inducements to buyers as other market centers, in the way of stocks they would draw fifty per cent. more business than they are now doing. We base this statement upon the fact that where large and complete stocks are carried, they are liberally patronized by interior merchants. Take as an illustration the house of

B. C. CLARK & CO.,

importers and jobbers of the different makes of crockery, china, glass and silverware, one of the most extensive and prosperous houses of the kind in the country. They have drawn the trade in their direction, simply because they are prepared to accommodate it to the fullest extent. And, as a result, their trade extends throughout the West, their stock offering the same advantages to buyers as do the largest houses at the East. In many instances during the past year interior merchants have either gone or sent to Chicago or St. Louis for their stocks, except crockery, glass and silverware, which they have bought here. Hence, we say, if wholesale dealers would imitate the example of Messrs. Clark & Co., and hold themselves ready to accommodate the trade to the fullest extent, the wholesale trade of Leavenworth would increase one-half during the next year. The engraving preceding these remarks is an exterior view of their wholesale house on Cherokee street, which is 65x285 feet. Besides which, they have a second house, 25x150 feet, of three floors, on Delaware street, where they carry an immense stock of all the finer grades of goods. This house was established in 1866, and its present trade approximates $300,000 per annum, with a healthy increase. They are both importers and wholesale dealers, and handle a full line of the most popular goods in their branch of trade, including silver-plated and brittania ware, table and pocket cutlery. They are also manufacturers' agents for Ohio stoneware. They also handle a full line of refrigerators and ice-boxes, including the "Palace," "Triumph," "Iceberg," "Ice-Chest," and "Jewett," all made at Buffalo. They employ fifteen salesmen in their store, and five traveling men on the road. The firm is composed of B. C. Clark, H. L. Clark, C. L. Knapp and J. H. E. Wiegant, all enterprising merchants, who, by competing with houses of the same kind at the East, in the way of stocks and prices, have deservedly secured one of the largest trades in the West.

THOMAS LEONARD,

wholesale and retail dealer in crockery, china, silver and glassware, at 420 Delaware street, also dates his citizenship back to 1857, previous to which, he was in business in Milwaukee, Wis. Mr. Leonard is a gentleman of good business views, and as he has been in commercial life for twenty-three years, the more distant readers of this work may be interested in learning what he thinks of Leavenworth. We give his own words: "In my opinion, the city is improving in its business. Trade in all channels is looking up. I, for one, would not change for Kansas City."

Mr. Leonard occupies a fine store, 54x70, carries an average stock of about $15,000, his sales amounting to about $50,000. His stock embraces everything in the line of plain and fancy crockery, china, glass and silverware, brittania, etc. His stock of fancy vases, lamps and chandeliers, is not surpassed by any house in the West, and right here the writer will say, in this line of goods country merchants can do as well here as in St. Louis or Chicago. They will find as large a stock, as great a variety, and the same range of prices as they will in the Eastern markets. Mr. Leonard has been in public life considerable since he became a resident here, having been, for four years—from 1870 to 1874—Sheriff of this county.

SEWING MACHINES.

Leavenworth being the chief center for the distribution of sewing machines in Kansas and adjoining States, all of the more popular makes of machines are represented by agencies here.

THE WHITE SEWING MACHINE,

which has been growing in public favor for the past three years, has a general distributing agency here, situated on the corner of Sixth and Shawnee streets, which is under the management of S. R. Shepherd, who has been in the sewing machine business for the past fifteen years, and he says "THE WHITE" is the best and most economical machine in the market, as it combines all of the valuable improvements in other machines besides its own original patent, which for solidity, simplicity and durability is unequaled. "THE WHITE" has been in the market about four years and they have already manufactured and sold over 150,000. There was fifty per cent. increase in the sales of this machine during 879. The average sales at this point is about 500 machines a year.

THE WHOLESALE GROCERY TRADE.

BITTMANN, TAYLOR & CO.,

the largest house of the kind in the State, and the oldest, was established in 1864. They employ six traveling salesmen, and their trade extends through Kansas into Colorado, Southern Nebraska, and to some extent, in New Mexico. The firm are both old citizens—Mr. Bittmann locating here in 1858, and Mr. Taylor in 1859. The former came here from Cincinnati, and the latter from New York, and both were engaged in the retail trade, previous to establishing their wholesale house. Their store is 50x125—three stories and basement, and their stock embraces a full line of staple and fancy groceries, and their books show an annual business of $1,000,000 to $1,200,000, with an average yearly increase of about twenty per cent. Thus it will be seen that their sales exceeds that of any other grocery house in the State.

Among the wholesale houses doing an extensive business in this city, is that of

ROHLFING & CO.,

importers and wholesale dealers in staple and fancy groceries, wines, liquors, fruits, cigars, etc., situated on the corner of Third and Cherokee streets. The house was established in 1858, and is among the oldest and most widely known business houses in the West, and we may add—for it is a fact—one of the most prosperous and solid. The firm were formerly in business in St. Louis, where they were favorably known as gentlemen of business breadth and enterprise. They occupy three floors—50x125—employ three salesmen in their store and one on the road, their annual sales averaging a half million dollars, and their trade extending to the mountains, west, and to the Gulf, south. Like all other old residents, they have the faith of a Universalist—that Leavenworth will develop into a great and prosperous business center.

THE RETAIL GROCERY TRADE.

In this channel of trade, Leavenworth has as many well-stocked houses as any city in the West. There are some twenty-four grocery houses—large and small—yet, the purpose of this chapter will be served, by mentioning a few of the largest, among which is that of

MICHAEL PHELAN,

who commenced the grocery trade on Fifth street, between Shawnee and Seneca streets, in 1864, and where he remained until 1866, when he secured a large store on the corner of Fifth and Seneca. His trade, however, continued to expand to such an extent, that in 1878, he secured two lots, 48x125 feet, on Shawnee, between Fifth and Sixth streets, on which he built the fine two-story structure he now occupies. The first story front is iron, the second story being of pressed brick, with white stone trimmings. The block is divided into two stores, communication between the two

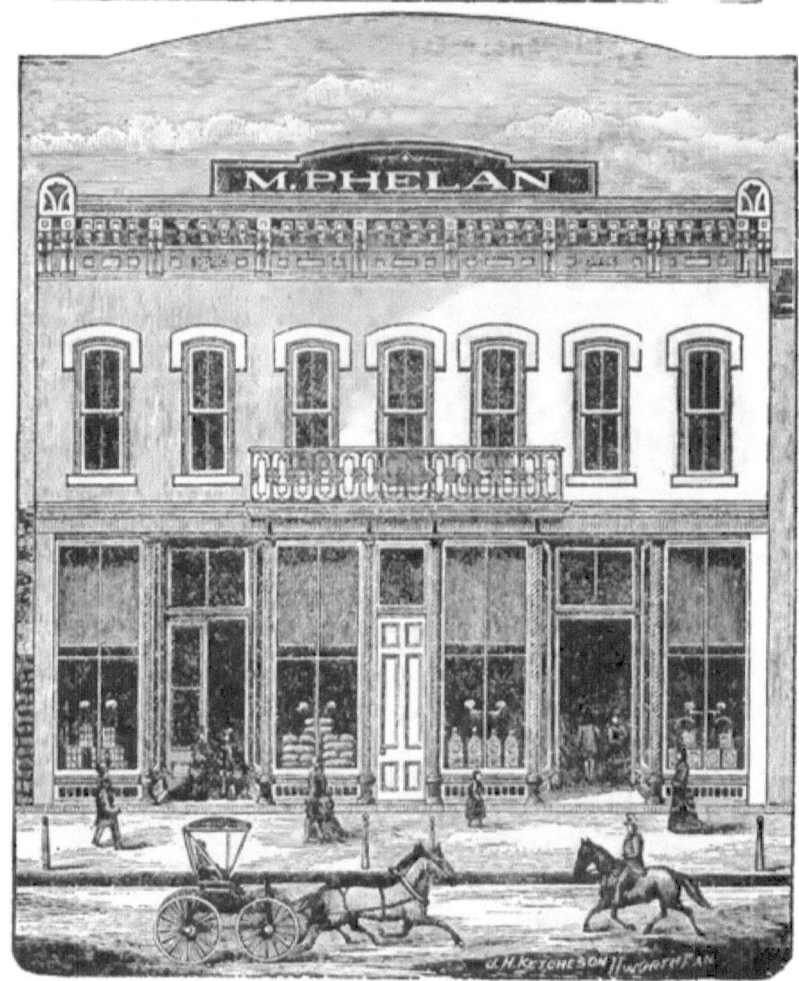

being by an imposing archway through the partition wall, near the centre of the building. Both of these stores, as also the basement, is occupied by Mr. Phelan. The east store, or right-hand store, as you face the building, is 24x100 feet, and is employed in handling staple and fancy groceries, where one of the largest and best selected stocks in the city will be found. The west store is 24x60 feet, and is used for handling provisions, flour and feed. To sum the whole matter up in a nut-shell, it is one of the best buildings on that street, and the most admirably arranged grocery house in the city. Mr. Phelan intends to finish off the second story for a residence for his family, which, when completed, will be commodious and pleasant. The cost of this building, exclusive of the ground, was something over $10,000, but it could not be built at the present time for less than $12,000. Mr. Phelan carries an averge stock of about $8,000, and his average annual sales are about $60,000. He employs five men and two teams, and delivers goods to all parts of the City and Fort.

Mr. Phelan is an enterprising, pleasant gentleman, and when it is stated that he commenced business here with only $1,500, the conclusion must be that he is an upright business man, who fully understands how to make the grocery trade popular with the public. Be that as it may, he is one of the solid and highly-esteemed business men of the city.

Adjoining Mr. Phelan's is the retail grocery house of

J. P. MARSHALL,

who has been a citizen of Leavenworth since 1856, and in the grocery trade since 1868. His store is 25x90 feet, and he carries an average stock of about $4,000. His stock embraces a full line of staple and fancy groceries, flour, feed and provisions. He has a large trade in choice roasted coffees. He is a pleasant gentleman to do business with, and is highly spoken of both in business and social circles.

On the northeast corner of Fifth and Shawnee streets, in the old market house, is situated the wholesale and retail grocery, glassware, crockery and liquor house of

AUGUST GENUIT,

who became a citizen here fourteen years ago, and who for the past eleven years has been engaged in his present business. His store is 50x50 feets and he carries an average stock of about $6,000, and his annual sale, ranges from $30,000 to $36,000. He employs three men and one team, and does business on the metropolitan system, his being one of the most popular grocery houses in the city. His motto is "fresh goods, quick sales, at small margins"—a system that has earned for him a large trade, and a popular standing in society.

ALEXANDER KIRK,

Retail grocer, and successor to W. S. Gable & Co., situated at 428 and 430 Cherokee street, is another of the many prosperous mercantile houses of the city. This house was started in 1868 by Garret & Kirk, Mr. Kirk taking the entire management in 1878. The establishment employs six clerks, delivery wagons, etc., and do a business of about $75,000 per annum. During our interview with Mr. Kirk he said: "I would take Leavenworth in preference to Kansas City for retail trade. I looked around considerable and at last decided to settle here, and I have never regretted the choice I made."

M. E. FRANK,

General dealer in staple and fancy groceries, canned goods, flour, provisions, etc., at 308 and 310 South Fifth street, has been a resident of the city for the past twenty-two years. He has a neat establishment and a good local trade, his sales averaging about $20,000 a year. When asked what he thought of Leavenworth he answered: "What should I think after living here twenty-two years? I think it is the best town in the West, the coal interest alone will make this a large city.

R. BEIGA—A general dealer in confectioneries, fruits, nuts, toys, tobacco and cigars, doing business at 310 Delaware street, has been a resident of this city for twenty-five years. He deals in ice cream, at wholesale and retail, and his parlors are very popular with the public. Mr. Beiga has been in the business twenty years and fully understands how to make that line of business popular.

WHOLESALE DRUGGISTS.

The wholesale drug interest is represented in this city by three houses. Prominent among these is the active and live drug house of

THEO. EGERSDORFF.

he occupies the two-story and basement structure, forty-eight feet front and ninety feet deep, on the northwest corner of Shawnee and Fourth streets. The corner room on Fourth street is used for a retail store. All the other rooms and basement are used for the wholesale business. This house was established in 1862, under the firm name of R. E. Watson & Co. Mr. Egersdorff assumed the entire management of the business in 1864. He employs ten men in his establishment. In addition to this force he has two men "on the road," their field of operation being Kansas, Missouri, Colorado and Iowa. The scientific pharmaceutical knowledge shown by this house, its fine business ability, and honorable fair dealing, has made for it a reputation second to no other house in the country.

ARNOLD & HUNT, WHOLESALE DRUGGISTS,

are situated on Delaware street, between Main and Second streets. The firm is composed of F. C. Arnold and F. R. Hunt, and commenced business three years ago. They occupy four floors, 24x125 feet, and without going into details, their stock includes everything generally carried by a first-class house of that kind, such as drugs, medicines, paints, oils, dyestuffs, chemicals, glass, liquors and wines for medical purposes. They do a business of $100,000 a year, and it is increasing 25 per cent a year. They speak highly of the business, both in its present and prospective outlook. Mr. Arnold has been a citizen here twenty years, and most of the time engaged in the drug trade. Mr. Hunt is also an old citizen and an enterprising business gentleman. They employ six salesmen in their store and two on the road.

On the southeast corner of Delaware and Fifth streets is the finely arranged drug store, the engraving of which is here given, of

GEO. C. VAUGHAN,

established in 1871 by B. E. Thompson, who sold the establishment to Mr. Vaughan sometime ago. Without any exaggeration it is the most elegantly fitted up drug store in the city, or as to that matter, in the West, The store is 30x100 feet. The floor is laid in diamond shaped marble tile, the only floor of the kind in the city. The counters, cases, and pannellings for the shelving are all of highly finished walnut, while the entire interior has a most inviting, tasty appearance. The stock carried is general and large, and embraces all goods usually found in a first-class drug store, such as imported and domestic drugs and druggist's supplies. Mr. Vaughan is a gentleman of experience and a practical chemist and druggist, and under his, and the previous management, the establishment has developed into one of the most popular prescription drug stores in the city. He handles nothing but drugs of ascertained purity and strength, and manufactures his own pharmaceutical preparations, such as elixirs fluid extracts, medicinal sirups, etc., a system which has added largely in extending his trade.

Among the popular prescription drug houses of the city, where prescriptions are carefully compounded day or night, is that of

MOONLIGHT,

situated on Fifth, between Shawnee and Delaware streets. Mr. Moonlight commenced the business in 1879, previous to which time he was for three years with Messrs. Campbell & Kendricks. He is of the "manner born" and a son of the present City Marshal, and has resided in Leavenworth for eighteen years. His stock is general, and embraces everything usually found in a first-class drug house, which he sells at low prices. He also carries a large and very complete line of Homeopathy remedies, his being one of the chief depots for that class of medicines in the State.

KANSAS MUSIC EMPORIUM.

CARL HOFFMAN.

In another portion of this work we made the statement that Leavenworth could point to the largest jewelry and hardware business in the West, and we will now add that she can boast of the largest wholesale and retail establishment for musical instruments and musical goods of any city west of the Mississippi. This is a pretty bold statement, but it is just as true as it is bold, as the writer has visited every city of any pretentions between Chicago and the Pacific, and in none has he seen a larger or better supplied establishment than that of Carl Hoffman of this city. In fact, it is the supply depot, as it were, for the more popular musical instruments and musical goods for the West. Mr. Hoffman's store is 25x125 feet, and throughout is a pattern of neatness and elegance. Besides his salesroom, he has a large warehouse on Shawnee street, where reserved stocks are stored. Mr. Hoffman came here from Pittsburg, Pennsylvania, in 1869, and his trade from that date has shown a healthy growth until now it averages about $75,000 per annum. He is the sole agent, West, for Chickering & Son's pianos; also for the Wilcox & White and Palace organs, instruments that have no superiors in the world. In brief, his stock embraces everything in the musical line found at metropolitan centers at the East. See inside front cover of this work.

THE FRUIT TRADE OF LEAVENWORTH.

A large per cent. of all fruits, domestic and foreign, consumed in Kansas and the immediate territory adjoining are distributed from this market, where that product is handled to a larger extent than at any other point west of the Missouri River. The house of

FARRELL BROS.,

which has been in business for the past fourteen years, and who handle the fruits both of this and other countries by car-load lots, have worked up an immense trade throughout the West. In breadth their operations cover the entire fields of fruits, nuts and confectioneries. The firm is composed of W. H. and J. H. Farrell, both having had an experience of

twenty-five years in that channel of commerce. Hence they fully under-
stand the obstacles encountered, and the frictions to be overcome in
handling perishable goods of that character successfully. Their establishment is commodious and admirably arranged for the business, and
with a full corps of employes carloads are unpacked, assorted, re-packed
and shipped to interior points with a most remarkable celerity. In brief,
with the prestige of large experience, they have been largely instrumental
in developing the fruit trade of the city to its present proportions. In
this, as in some other channels of the wholesale trade, where in quantity,
quality and prices, stocks offer equal advantages to buyers with other
large markets, Leavenworth seldom gets the go-by from Western buyers,
for it is no more a fact that supply and demand govern values than
that trade will flow in directions where it meets with the best accommodations. And the fruit houses here, as also such other branches of the
wholesale trade as handle stocks equal to the most extended demand,
fully warrants the opinion that if stocks in every wholesale house were
doubled, the demand would immediately respond by a corresponding
increase. In expressing their views on Leavenworth in its present and
prospective, Messrs. Farrell said: "There is a perceptible improvement
in all channels of trade. There are no desirable business houses vacant,
all are occupied and new ones are being built. Old manufacturers are
increasing their productive capacity and new and important ones are
locating here. Leavenworth has many elements of advantage not found
in other Western cities. The abundant supply of cheap fuel is an advantage that no amount of competition can wrest from her. Then again, the
social elements, the religious and educational advantages, the healthful
condition and the beautiful location of the city, are all powerful factors in
drawing people in this direction."

TOBACCO AND CIGARS.

As in all other mercantile channels, the tobacco and cigar trade is
represented by as solid and prosperous houses as will be found in the
West. A leading house in this line, is that of

ROTHENBERG & SCHLOSS,

located at 302 Delaware street, commenced business here in 1870. Mr.
Rothenberg was formerly in business at Hartford, Connecticut, while
Mr. Schloss was educated to the business in New York, although both
gentlemen have resided in Leavenworth for sixteen years. They carry a
large stock of cigars, tobacco and smoking goods generally — handling, as
a specialty, the leading brands of choice cigars made at Cincinnati, New
York, and other eastern markets; also, a full line of imported goods. They
keep three salesmen on the road, and do an annual business of $125,000—
their trade covering a good portion of Kansas and adjoining States. Their
ten-cent "Monagram" "Old Judge," and "Hand-made Havana" cigars
are favorites in the West; while their popular five centers include "Foun-
tain Head" and "Old Rose."

MILLER & MILLER,

Who have been citizens of Leavenworth since the days of its infancy,
although they established their present business only three years since.
They carry a good assortment of cigars, tobacco and smoking goods, and
manufacture several favorite brands of cigars. They do a business of
about $3,000 a year, and are both industrious, enterprising gentlemen.

ISAAC REACH—General dealer in clothing, gentlemen's furnishing
goods, boots and shoes, harness and saddles, who does a business of
$20,000 a year, came to this city from Savannah, Ga., in 1868. He
employs five workmen, and makes a specialty in manufacturing tents,
wagon covers harness and saddles of all descriptions. He is ener-
getic in business, square in his dealings and is deserving of the liberal
patronage he is receiving.

THE LEAVENWORTH TIMES,

of which D. R. Anthony—than whom no newspaper man West of St. Louis is better known—is proprietor, was established in 1857. Although a staunch Republican journal, in all instances of indecency, rascality and crime, it has invariably hewed to the line in the interest of the public, regardless of who the chips may strike, or in other words, it does not allow party fealty to stand in the way of exposing political wrongs, crop out where they may, when the interests of the public are at stake. The Times issues a daily and weekly edition, each having a larger circulation than any other newspaper in the State, which shows its popularity and usefulness.

The Times building, a fine brick structure, 48x110 feet, three stories and basement, is by far the most admirably arranged and best equipped printing house West of St. Louis. The building extends from Main street through to the Levee, being two stories in height on the first-named thoroughfare, and three stories and basement on the Levee. The basement proper is employed as an engine room. On the next floor is the book and job office, where five first-class power printing presses, a folding machine and other approved appliances for executing first-class work—all under the supervision of W. C. Hinman—are kept constantly at work.

On the first floor of the Main street front is the counting room, private office and library of Col Anthony, stock room and a finely-arranged reading room, the vestibule fronting the counting room being fitted up with racks and tables for that purpose, and on which are found all of the more popular publications of the day. The rooms on this floor are admirably arranged and elegantly fitted up and furnished. On the second floor are the editorial and composing rooms. The Times employs forty-five men. W. S. Burke occupying the editorial chair—a position he has ably filled for the past nine years. Will Van Benthusen, an experienced journalist, fills the position of night editor, and superintends the telegraph and news columns. N. B. Perry is at the head of the local department, where he has so successfully superintended the dishing up of local events for the past four years. The cash box of the establishment is under the control of Frank T. Lynch, who has occupied the position of business manager for the establishment for the past six years, and without the least desire to inflict a puff on the young gentleman, we will say that the prosperity of The Times is in a large measure due to his careful and judicious management of its finances.

Terms:—Daily Times, a thirty-two column folio sheet, $8.00 per annum. Weekly Times, a forty-eight column quarto sheet, $1.25 a year.

HARDWARE AND CUTLERY.

This interest is well represented in Leavenworth by one of the largest and oldest wholesale establishment of the kind west of St. Louis. We refer to the house of

J. F. RICHARDS & CO.,

Established by Mr. Richards in 1856, when Leavenworth was in its swaddling clothes. J. W. Park, the junior partner, has been identified with the interests of the house since 1867, and a member of the firm since 1877. The house has had a steady growth of business for years, its sales for 1879 showing a large increase over the previous year, and a larger increase the present year. They occupy two stores, one at 209 and the

other at 302 Delaware street, both three story and basement structures, 25 x 125 feet. The first is used as a warehouse and the second for wholesaling. Their specialties are heavy hardware, European and American cutlery, nails, iron and steel. They have the largest house in Kansas City, where they also carry a very large stock of the same line of goods. They are Western agents for the Fairbank's scale, also for Macauley & Urban burglar proof safes. If one should give ear to the envious reports circulated against Leavenworth by some of her Western sister cities, a wholesale house of the business dimensions of Messrs.

Richards & Co.'s would be looked upon with astonishment. Leavenworth has never indulged in blowing her own bugle to any extent, notwithstanding the fact she has the largest flouring mills, the largest stove works, the largest wagon factory, the largest hardware house, the largest jewelry house, the most extensive coal mines, the largest furniture houses, and withal, the largest number of solid business men of any town west of St. Louis. But to return to Messrs. Richards & Co., their trade extends throughout the West and is keeping even pace with the growth of the country. And what gives them a prestige, is, they have both the means and ability to supply the demand as advantageously as the larger Eastern houses.

J. W. CRANCER

Is another of the solid business men of Leavenworth, who scores a mercantile record of twenty-two years in the city. He has watched its developments from a mere hamlet to a city of 25,000 people, and has always had a shoulder to the wheel of its advancement, and now, as a reward for his fealty, he enjoys a trade of fully $60,000 a year in stoves and general hardware and a high reputation financially and socially. "You ask my opinion as to the past, present and future of Leavenwosth," said Mr. Crancer. "The past has been a checkered one, prosperity and adversity being about equal in the balance. The past, however, opens a field altogether too wide for valuable suggestions at this time. In the present, in my opinion, we are entering a prosperous era, which clothes the future with the most hopeful promises. I have watched the progress of Leavenworth as closely as any one, and I do not hesitate in saying that business prospects to-day are brighter than they have been for years. Examine our business interests and you will find that every man who has stood by the town is doing a prosperous business. Sir, there is no better point for manufacturing or merchandizing business in the West than this."

FRED A. MILLER,

hardware merchant, on the corner of Delaware and Firth streets, may not have been the first white man that settled in this city, yet he must have come pretty near it, as he was here and in this vicinity since 1851, when there was nothing but a Government post where the city now stands. He was formerly a resident of Missouri, and established in business here in 1863. Besides his house here, Mr. Miller has an establishment of the same kind in Kansas City. He carries a general stock of hardware, builders' hardware, tools, nails, glass, pumps, pump material, etc. He also carries one of the largest stocks of wire screen goods to be found in the city. He has an average trade of about $30,000 per annum.

B. S. RICHARDS,

wholesale and retail dealer in harness and saddlery goods and saddlery hardware, and now doing a business of from $40,000 to $50,000 per annum, commenced trade here in 1861. He employs twenty-five men, and m akes a specialty of handling goods at wholesale, in which departmen the has a large trade throughout the West. Mr. Richards is one of the oldest and most reliable business men of the city, and as his opinion will have weight, we will employ his own words: "In my opinion, an era of prosperity has set in for our city. The outside world just begin to realize that it is the best point for investing capital in manufacturing enterprises west of the Mississippi River. One thing is certain: all of the substantial business men who staid in the city instead of leaving it when the hard times overtook us, are the solid, prosperous men of the city to-day. Leavenworth has railways enough for its wholesale and retail trade, and as her manufacturing resources are developed, her railway facilities will increase."

STOVES, TINNERS' STOCK, ETC.

G. H. LUDOLPH,

manufacturer of tin, sheet-iron and copper ware ; also, general dealer in stoves, china and earthen ware, situated at No. 226 Shawnee street, is one of the pioneer merchants of the city, having come here when one could successfully hunt rabbits in places where some portions of the business heart of the city now stands. He is one of the oldest and best known hardware merchants in the city, and his stock embraces nearly everything in the hardware and crockery line, including glass, crockery, cutlery, etc. His stock of stoves, iron, copper, tin, Japan and marbelized ware is large. He makes roofing, cornices and guttering a specialty, and does all descriptions of job work in tin, copper and sheet iron. In brief, he keeps pace with the improvements of the day, and is always ready to supply customers with anything in the hardware line. He employs three men, carries an average stock of about $3,000, and his sales average about $6,000 a year. An honest heart and willing hands have made made him one of the solid merchants here.

Among the well-known business men who came to Leavenworth at an early day, is

B. KORMAN,

general dealer in stoves, hardware, tin, sheet-iron and copper goods, at No. 402 Shawnee street. Mr. Korman came to this country from Poland in 1855, and to this city in 1859 — his capital consisting chiefly of industrious hands and an honest, strong heart. The city was then a mere hamlet, where now stands a proud, commercial town of twenty-five thousand people, and we find that Mr Korman has also undergone a change. He is now the owner of a fine two-story brick store, 25x65 feet, carries an average stock of $5,000, and sells about $18,000 a year. He manufactures all kinds of tin, sheet iron and copper goods — making a specialty of roofing, guttering and all job work, to which end he employs six experienced workmen. In conclusion, we will say: "Mr. Korman is an enterprising gentleman, who has done his share toward building up Leavenworth."

JULIUS MINCKE,

dealer in hardware, is located on the corner of Fifth and Cherokee streets. He came from Germany in 1870, and established his business the following year. His store is 60x25 feet, and is well filled with the different kinds and grades of hardware, cutlery, nails, glass, mechanics' tools, scales, presses and builders' material. He is also agent for the celebrated "Boston" tools. His motto has been "quick sales and small profits," and by fair dealing and strict attention to business, he has built up a retail trade of $20,000.

FIRE ARMS AND SPORTING GOODS.

JOHN BIRINGER,

manufacturer of all kinds of fire arms, and general dealer in sporting goods, including the different makes of rifles, shot-guns, pistols, ammunition, fishing tackle, etc.—in fact, his stock includes all articles in the sporting goods line. Mr. Biringer commenced trade here about twenty-one years ago, previous to which time he was in the same line of business in Philadelphia. He sells goods at the same range of prices as charged in St. Louis or Chicago.

PHOTOGRAPHIC ARTIST.

As the good book says, "their name is legion," but artists that have made it a life-time study are not legion. There are plenty in the profession who can take the different kinds of pictures regardless of their similarity to the subject, but those who can portray on the card-board the likeliness of a person, are few. What we mean by the likeliness is this: the natural expression of the face, the natural and easy position of the body, also the true expression of the eyes; then combined with all this, the finishing process is what constitutes the true artistic skill. Now, in order to do this work successfully, one must, in the first place, be a natural artist, then it takes long years of study and practical experience to be master of the business. Mr. Henry, who has been in Leavenworth for the past fourteen years, and is located at 322 Delaware street, we find is a natural artist, and has made it a life study. In all the arts in this and the Old World the progress in this art has been second to none of the others; and, judging from the interior of Mr. Henry's studio, we find he has kept pace with the times. He has the sole right in Leavenworth for the lightning negative process, which is very desirable for those who wish to have pictures of small children, as it only takes two seconds for a negative. He also makes a specialty of the celebrated panel photographs, which are so popular at the present time. In order to maintain his well-earned reputation for doing the best work in the West, he has engaged one of the best artists from the East, who has been with him for over a year, and he does not have to send his work away to have it retouched. We would say in closing: for first-class work and reasonable prices, call on Mr. Henry at his old stand.

FLOWERS, BOUQUETS, ETC.

H. S. NORTON.

We find that Mr. Norton came here in 1872, and has had eight years' experience in the business. He has three large green-houses, two of them being 11x75 feet, and the third 18x50 feet. His stock includes all kinds of green-house plants, roses, bulbs, etc., and he is prepared to furnish boquets, wreaths, crosses, and in fact every description of cut flowers at short notice. His grounds are located on the corner of Cherokee and Second streets.

WHOLESALE AND RETAIL FRUIT HOUSE.

H. M. TANNER,

General commission merchant and wholsale dealer in domestic and foreign fruits, proaduce, etc., established the business in 1875, although he has been a resident of the city and State for the past twenty-five years. As an index to the breadth of his trade, we will say that he occupies four floors, 25x110 feet, and transacts an annual business of from $50,000 to $55,000. He handles on an average 250 car loads of apples a year, his trade extending throughout the Western States and Territories. He employs six men. Being one of the active, prominent busines men of the city, whose views will have weight, we asked his opinion as to future business prospects, to which he responded: " I think the business interests of Leavenworth are on a solid footing, and based, as they are, on a manufacturing industry that, is growing in importance, the mercantile interests, both in a wholesale and retail way, must increase in breadth and prosperity. As our manufacturing advantages become more generally known, capital will flow in this direction for profitable investment.

The engraving heading these remarks represents the confectionery and fruit house of

A. BEIGA,

located at 422 Delaware street. Mr. Beiga has been engaged in the business for many years, and is too well known throughout the entire West to require any commendatory remarks at our hands. By manufacturing and handling pure, reliable goods, and upright dealing, he has deservedly earned a business and reputation that no amount of competition can wrest from him. His retail trade extends throughout the city and country, while his wholesale traffic is co-extensive with the Western States and Territories. Mr. Beiga is an experienced, pleasant gentleman to do business with.

At No. 225 Delaware street, is situated the Trunk Factory of

P. J. FRELING,

who commenced business here some thirteen years ago, previous to which, he was in business in Chicago. He occupies two floors and a basement, 24x95 feet — the first floor being used as a salesroom for trunks, valises, traveling bags, ladies' and gentlemen's satchels and baskets. In brief, he carries a full line of the better class of goods usually found in first-class houses of that kind. The second floor is employed as a factory for trunks and valises, and the basement for storage. Mr. Freling is an enterprising business gentleman, and he has secured a good trade throughout the West. In regard to the future trade ot the city, he said to the waiter: "In my estimation, the future never looked more promising for business than at the present time.

WINN'S BAZAAR—Of which an account is given in another part of this work, is one of the most popular places in the city.

HATS, CAPS AND FURS.

In reading this work it will be seen that a large per cent. of the prosperous business men of Leavenworth have been citizens of the place from ten to twenty-five years.

MR. PH. ROTHSCHILD,

General dealer in fashionable hats, caps and furs, at 304 Delaware street, is one of the number. He located here in 1855, a quarter of a century ago, and in 1862 organized his present business, which has steadily increased until the present time, when his sales average about $45,000 a year. He occupies two floors, 25x80 feet, carries a large stock of the different popular styles of hats and caps, keeps two traveling men on the road and his trade extends throughout the West. "Yes," said Mr. Rothschild, "I have lived here for twenty-five years constantly; I have stuck to the town through its days of prosperity and adversity; I have always predicted that it would be the largest and most prosperous city in the State, and the present shows that my predictions are realized."

MISCELLANEOUS.

M. A. KELLY,

manufacturer of brooms, and wholesale dealer in broom-corn and broom material, has been in business here for five years, and now he manufactures, on an average, sixty dozen brooms per week, for all of which he finds a ready market, and his trade is steadily increasing. His brooms are equal in quality to any manufactured in the country, as he selects his corn with great care, and employs only the most skillful workmen. He uses about forty tons of corn per annum, and gives employment to seven men. He said: "I think the town is improving. It is much better for my business than when I first came here."

JAMES FOLEY

commenced business here in 1876. He is a plumber, gas and steam fitter, and has a high reputation. Mr. Foley has devoted his life thus far to the trade, and to meet the demand, employs six reliable workmen, and does an average business of $8,000 a year. He also deals largely in pumps, lead and wrought-iron pipe, brass-work, gas fixtures, bath tubs, wash basins, kitchen sinks, rubber hose, etc. He makes a specialty of fitting buildings with water, gas and steam pipes, and furnishes estimates for parties in city or country when desired. His store is at 220 Delaware street, and is 25x80 feet. He said: "I was in business at Atchison for some time, but I find Leavenworh a far better town for trade." Mr. Foley is agent for and handles the "Victor" self-governing wind mill — one of the best in use. He also handles lightning rods, and fills orders both for city and country.

GEORGE A. FOY,

dealer in new and second-hand furniture, and all kinds of house furnishing goods, came to Leavenworth in 1857 and established his present business. He is located at 202, 204 and 206 North Fifth street — his store being 60x55. Although he handles second-hand goods, he also has facilities for buying and selling everything in the line of new furniture, and does so at prices that defy competition. His stock of goods comprise everything that is necessary to the furnishing of a house in the line of stoves, crockery, glassware, and a full line of carpetings.

J. F. BRINK—General dealer in toys, school books and stationery, on North Fifth street, between Shawnee and Seneca streets, carries a fine stock and is doing a good business.

HERMAN RICHTER,

dealer in furniture, window shades, and upholsterer, commenced business here in 1878, previous to which time, for sixteen years, he was engaged in the same business in Chicago. He occupies three floors, 22x100 feet, and employs six skilled workmen, and his trade in 1879 reached $6,000. He is a young man possessing those elements of energy and industry so necessary to success. He carries a full stock of goods in his line, and makes a specialty of custom work.

HENRY DECKELMAN,

jeweler at 226 Delaware street, dates his citizenship here back twenty-three years. He occupies a store 22x80 feet, has a well selected stock of jewelry, watches, etc. He manufactures and repairs, in which line he enjoys a high reputation. He makes a specialty of the "Boss Filled Case," and does a business of about $50,000 per annum. He said: "I have full faith in the prosperity of Leavenworth, and have always had, or I would have gone elsewhere years ago."

CARPET MILLS.

Leavenworth has a carpet mill, of which John Scott, a practical carpet weaver, from Scotland, is proprietor, and it is the only establishment west of Philadelphia where two-ply carpets are woven. Mr. Scott has twelve looms, although at the present time he only operates two. He manufactures a fine grade of two-ply carpet, and as he competes with Eastern goods, his trade is increasing. This is an industry in which capital could be employed to an advantage in this city.

W. D. SKINNER,

Dealer in all kinds of furniture, 526 and 523 Shawnee street, came to Leavenworth in 1876 from Illinois, where he learned the furniture business. After working at the furniture trade three years, he opened a store for himself, in 1879, and to-day is doing a prosperous business. He buys and sells both new and second hand furniture and household goods of all kinds. He showed the writer a black walnut set for $65, that for durability and finish could not be bought for a penny less in Chicago. His store is 50x39 feet, and he buys all his goods in white and finishes them himself. Said Mr. Skinner: "When I came to Leavenworth I had five dollars in my pocket, and to-day I am doing a fair business and own all my stock of goods."

A GRAVE SUBJECT.

The mattock, coffin and melancholy grave, are not cheerful subjects to contemplate, and yet, coffins, caskets and undertakers are as much a commercial necessity as anything else in this world; hence, that channel of trade must take its place in this work. There are two undertaker establishments in this city, that of

J. B. DAVIS & CO.,

on Delaware street, between Fourth and Fifth streets which was established in 1855, being the oldest and largest. Their stock embraces all goods in that line, from the finest casket to the most common burial case. Their facilities and equipages for conducting funerals, are the best in the West. They do an average business of $6,000 per annum. They are gentlemen of broad business views ; they said to the writer : "We think this one of the most advantageous points on the Missouri for manufacturing and wholesaling. We were here during the days of 'Border Ruffianism,' and the rebellion, and have watched events during the days of cloud and sunshine, and never saw brighter prospects for the town than there are to-day."

AUCTION AND COMMISSION.

If ever, by choice or chance, the distant reader should visit Leavenworth, and have occasion to pass down Delaware street, he or she, as the case may be. will be attracted by the auction sales that occur every day at the establishment of

D. A. HOOK & CO.,

located at No. 418 on the thoroughfare named. The business is only about two years old, and yet their sales for 1879 were over $75,000. They handle goods both on commission and at auction. The firm is composed of D. A. and Enos Hook, both of which have a citizenship of twenty-four years, having settled here in 1857. D. A. Hook served the public as United States Marshal for nine years, and as City Marshal for five years, while Enos, his brother, is now filling his second term as Treasurer of Leavenworth county. In speaking of Leavenworth, Mr. D. A. Hook said: "In my opinion, we are entering a prosperous era. At all events, the feeling to-day is better here in Leavenworth than it ever was before."

E. HENSLEY,

general commission merchant on Main, between Delaware and Shawnee streets, has been a resident of Leavenworth for twenty-three years. He is a highly esteemed citizen, and as an evidence that he is reliable, it is only necessary to state that he does a business of $2,500 per month. He handles all descriptions of goods and produce on commission. He said to the writer: "Leavenworth done business on the 'hot-bed' system until after the war, and since then many have been induced to leave the place owing to high taxes and other causes. We are, however, now growing into a solid business town, especially in manufacturing. There is a healthy and solid improvement prevalent on all sides. The opportunities for the investment of capital here I consider excellent.

LIVERY AND FEED STABLES.

THE NEW OPERA HOUSE LIVERY STABLES,

of which H. L. S. McLanathan is proprietor, are really the largest and best arranged of any in the City. Mr. McLanathan has $10,000 invested in the business, has had an experience of thirty years, and hence understands what is required to make an institution of that kind popular. His stock includes fifty head of horses, and thirty carriages and buggies. It is a boarding and sale stable also, and has excellent accommodations for one hundred head of horses. The building is 72x125 feet — three stores — and is admirably arranged. Mr. McL. has some fine turnouts, and makes a specialty of funerals and parties. "You ask my opinion of Leavenworth," said Mr. McLanathan: "I can tell you, in a few words. The prospects of the town to-day are better than they have been for ten years, both in mercantile and manufacturing channels. And until an excellent climate, good society and cheap rents, with an abundance of cheap fuel loose their value, the city will continue to expand."

THE MANSION HOUSE LIVERY STABLES,

of which W. T. Woods & Son are proprietors, are situated on Shawnee, between Fifth and Sixth streets, were established in 1878. Their stock includes eleven good horses, six buggies and two carriages. They have $3,500 invested, and a trade of about $5,500 a year. W. T. Woods has been a citizen of the city and county since 1866. After locating here, he first engaged in the livery business, but afterwards turned his attention to farming, which he followed until 1878, when he returned to the city and formed the present co-partnership with his son, who fills the position of book-keeper for Messrs. Keith & Henry, of Kansas City. They combine the livery, boarding and sale of stock, and their establishment is well patronized, and its trade is expanding.

THE LIVE STOCK INTEREST.

There is, at the present time, about 6,000 head of hogs, 6,000 head of cattle, and about the same number of sheep marketed in Leavenworth annually. There are two small stock yards in the city — one on the corner of Broadway and Shawnee streets, and the other, between Cherokee and Choctaw streets. These yards are arranged so as to comfortably accommodate two hundred head of cattle at a time. These yards are owned by E. T. Latta, an old stock man, who has been in business since 1869. He also has the management of the stock yards, which are owned by the Rock Island, and Missouri Pacific Railways. Mr. Latta is also the proprietor of the feed and sale stables for horses, connected with tha first-named yards.

MEAT MARKETS.

JOHN VOLZ,

One of the largest wholesale and retail dealers in fresh and salt meats in the city, is located at 738 and 740 Shawnee street. He has been in business ten years, and his sales average about $125,000 a year. He furnishes a large amount of meats for Ft. Leavenworth, also for other Government posts to the southwest. Mr. Volz was in the same business for ten years in St. Louis, before locating here. His establishment is the best supplied, and most popular, in the city; and, as a result, his trade is rapidly increasing. In short, it is one of the solid, prosperous business houses of Leavenworth.

MARTIN HELLER,

on the corner of Broadway and Shawnee streets, is another well supplied, popular meat market. The structure is a fine two-story brick, built and owned by Mr. Heller, who has been in the meat business in this city for the past thirteen years. His market is one of the finest and best arranged in this city; and, as he handles the best qualities of meat, it is a popular place to buy. He does an average business of about $6,000 a year, and his trade is increasing from month to month.

THE MOLINE PLOW COMPANY, Moline, Ill.,

manufacturers of the finest quality of cast-steel plows, cultivators, sulkies, harrows and scrapers.

THE MOLINE SULKY has made the best record of any sulky ever introduced.

Catalogues, circulars, price lists and a handsome chromo illustrating the MOLINE AT WORK sent free to any address.

Dealers who wish territory for the best selling implements made should write for terms and prices.

PERSONAL NOTICES.

CAPT. H. L. BICKFORD.

general contractor, is a man who has been for many years prominent in the affairs of the city, and is generally known to the public men of the State. He has been in the City Council, State Legislature, and has many times been called by his fellow citizens to the discharge of responsible public duties, acquitting himself at all times with credit to himself and his constituents. He is an enterprising public-spirited man, and during all the many years of his residence in Leavenworth he has always been ready and willing to take an active part in any public enterprise.

The Kansas Pump Manufacturing Company,

on Shawnee street, near Sixth street, have a large variety of pumps and pump material.

PARTIES visiting this City, and desiring to secure pleasant furnished rooms convenient to the business heart of the City, will find such by applying to Mrs. M. Heath, at 612 Delaware street.

NEWSPAPERS OF LEAVENWORTH.

There are three daily papers printed in this City—two American and one German—and six weeklies, besides several monthly publications, the most important among the latter being the *Western Homestead*, edited and published by W. S. Burke and D. A. Beckwith, both practical newspaper men of enterprise and ability.

THE LEAVENWORTH TIMES.

of which D. R. Anthony is editor and proprietor, ranks both in influence and circulation as the leading Republican organ of the State. THE TIMES owns one of the finest and best arranged newspaper, book and job offices west of St. Louis. Both the daily and weekly issues of THE TIMES has a larger circulation than any other publications in Kansas. It exhibits more enterprise, is conducted with more ability, and is the most prosperous journal in the West. It is to Kansas and the West, what the Chicago *Tribune* is to its area of circulation.

THE LEAVENWORTH PRESS,

an evening daily, of which G. A. Atwood is editor and proprietor, was started in 1872. It is the official paper of the city and county and in ability and breadth of character may be classed among the leading Republican prints of the State. Mr. Atwood came to Iowa from Vermont, his native State, in 1867. His first Western newspaper experience was in conducting the Dallas (Iowa) *Gazette*, which he bought immediately after reaching that State, and which he edited and published for some four years. In 1871 he disposed of the *Gazette* and went to Boston, in which, as in other parts of New England, he spent about one year, when he again returned to the West and started the Ellsworth *Reporter*, in this State, which he conducted with marked ability. Under his management the *Reporter* was one of the most popular weekly prints in the State, and its circulation is said to have exceeded that of any other weekly journal west of Topeka. After disposing of the Ellsworth *Reporter* and previous to purchasing the *Press* he published the Kansas *Monthly*. Mr. Atwood is an easy and forcible writer, and under his able management the *Press* is rapidly increasing the scope of its usefulness.

"THE WORKINGMAN'S FRIEND."

On the 16th day of November, 1878, James W. Remington, a practical printer and newspaper man, issued the first number of the *The Workingman's Friend*. He had the hearty endorsment of the laboring party of the city and county, which was very strong. The paper has from that day to this been growing, both in size and patronage. The paper was small at the beginning, being a five column sheet, but the untiring energy of the proprietor has made it a paying institution, and from time to time he has been compelled to enlarge until now it is as pretty a forty-eight column weekly as one often sees. The paper is well printed, neatly made up and shows upon its very face the work of a practical man. It is what we term a *family paper*, filled each week with the choicest of reading, stories, poetry, condensed telegraphic news, market reports, miscellaneous matter, local news and editorial topics upon all important subjects.

APPEAL AND TRIBUNE,

a well printed, forty column quarto weekly, now in its tenth year, is edited and published by P. B. Castle, who previous to engaging in the nwspaper business, was quite prominently connected with the insurance interests in this State. It is ostensibly an Independent sheet, and as such has a large and fruitful field of operations. Independent journalism in this country, when conducted with that high sense of honor and dignity that should characterize all neutral prints, must prove prosperous and useful.

THE KANSAS FREIE PRESSE.

is the only German daily paper published in the State, and of which Haberlein & Bro. are editors and proprietors, is now in its thirteenth year of usefulness. It issues both a daily and weekly edition, each having a large circulation. Its typography is excellent, and its management shows breadth of character and ability.

AN IMPORTANT INVENTION.

One of the most important and useful inventions of the age, is what is known as the French Motor Sewing Machine, recently introduced to the public in this country, and for which arrangements have been made for manufacturing in this City by enterprising parties from Chicago and St. Louis. The LEAVENWORTH TIMES, in its issue of the 30th of June last, in speaking of this new candidate for public favor says :

"For several days past parties from Chicago and St. Louis have been in the City, arranging the details for locating here an establishment for manufacturing what is known as the

FRENGH-AMERICAN MOTOR SEWING MACHINE,

or, in other words, the French Motor for Sewing Machines of all makes. 'The Motor' is an invention of Cyrus and Napleon Du Bruel, of France, and is of recent date, and that it is destined to become a most important factor in the Sewing Machine industry there is scarcely a shadow of doubt, We shall not attempt a description of this important invention, further than to say that it entirely overcomes the 'dead center' impediment universal in all crank motions; renders it impossible to propel the machine the wrong way; makes the machine run one-half lighter, and increases its motion to 1,000 stitches per minute. But the great importance of the improvement is in the fact that it entirely relieves the operative from all injurious effects of muscular strain, so common with the ordinary Sewing Machine.

"'The Motor' can be seen in operation at the White Sewing Machine Depot, on the corner of Shawnee and Sixth streets, and as its proprietors have decided to manufacture them here, our citizens should examine its merits, and if deserving of their endorsement, should welcome the new enterprise with open arms."

STATISTICAL.

Number of Buildings in Leavenworth.

The number of buildings within the corporate limits of Leavenworth, on the 1st day of May, 1880, were 4,686. Of this number, 1,728 are built of brick, stone and iron, and the remainder of wood.

The Leading Commerce of Leavenworth for 1879.

In compiling the following statistics, actual figures have in most instances been obtained, and while our aggregates may not be exact to a dollar, for all practical purposes they are correct.

Sales of Merchandise for 1879.

Dry Goods,	$ 849,000
Millinery Goods,	151,216
Clothing and Furnishing Goods,	646,487
Boots, Shoes and Leather,	589,942
Groceries and Provisions,	2,397,867
Hardware and Cutlery,	412,364
Stoves, Tinware, etc.,	226,179
Musical Instruments, etc.,	116,418
Jewelry and Silverware, etc.,	418,918
Crockery, Glassware, etc.,	329,316
Fancy Goods, Notions and Toys,	174,219
Fire Arms, Sporting Goods, etc.,	92,316
Drugs, Medicines, Paints, Oils, etc.,	409,727
Wines and Liquors,	467,847
Beer and Ale,	87,219
Tobacco, Cigars, etc.,	319,812
Furniture and Carpets,	682,737
Agricultural Implements and Seeds,	226,211
Wagons and Carriages,	674,384
Lumber and Building Materials,	527,487
Engines, Boilers, Mill and other Machinery,	356,472
Flour and Feed,	947,319
Cigar, Paper and Fancy Boxes,	31,164
Barbers' Supplies,	15,000
Marble, Granite, Stone, etc.,	59,847
Books, Stationery, etc.,	325,314
Fruits, Confectionery, etc.,	237,217
Woolens manufactured here,	60,000
Hats and Caps,	116,000
Sewing Machines,	54,860
Cotton and Paper Bags,	84,911
Soaps manufactured here,	20,000
Harness, Saddles, Horse Collars, etc.,	187,379
Coal and Wood,	2,847,849
Total,	$11,043,698

There are a score or more of industries not included in the above, such as carpet weaving, broom making, lock making and brass manufacturing, where we were unable to secure information as to the amount of business transacted.

Creative Wealth.

The wealth created by the manufacturing industries of Leavenworth, for the year 1879, was, in round numbers, two million, three hundred and thirty-seven thousand dollars, with an increase of about 20 per cent. thus far for 1880.

THT BUSINESS INDUSTRIES OF LEAVENWORTH.

The following is a statement of the number of the different business industries in this City:

Attornies at Law................48	Hardware and Cutlery............... 6
Abstract of Title Offices.............. 3	Hats and Caps................... 3
Architects................. 5	Hides and Wool, etc................ 3
Ammunition and Fire Arms......... 2	Hot Air Furnaces................ 1
Agricultural Implements............ 5	Hotels................ 8
Artists................. 6	Harness Makers................... 8
Banks. 3	Hair Workers................... 2
Bakeries 7	Ice Dealers................ 7
Bag Manufactory................. 1	Insurance Agents................15
Barber Supply Factory.......... 1	Insurance Companies, (Fire) Branch
Barbers................16	Offices......................43
Broom Factories.................. 2	Insurance Companies, (Life)......... 6
Basket Factory................ 1	Iron and Steel................ 3
Books and Stationery.. 8	Justices of the Peace.............. 4
Book Binders.................. 3	Liquor Dealers................10
Boiler Works.................. 1	Livery Stables.. 14
Billiard Halls................ 4	Lumber Dealers. 5
Boot and Shoe Dealers............35	Marble Works................... 2
Box Factories................. 2	Mattrass Makers................ 5
Bill Posters................... 2	Meat Markets................17
Breweries 4	Mercantile Agencies.............. 2
Beer Bottlers 2	Millinery and Fancy Goods. 6
Brass Foundries.................. 2	Milliner and Dress Makers.........18
Blacksmiths................12	Musical Instruments............. 3
Bleachers of Straw Goods.......... 3	Newspapers................... 7
Boarding Houses................23	Omnibus Lines................ 2
Cabinet Makers.............. 8	Oysters, Fish and Game........... 4
Carpenters and Builders..............16	Packing Houses................ 3
Carpet Mills................. 1	Painters, (House and Sign) 8
Carpet and Oil Cloth.............. 3	Pawn Brokers................ 2
Carriage and Wagon Material....... 2	· Photographers (See Artists)
Carriage and Wagon Factories......... 6	Physicians.....................27
China and Glassware.......... 2	Planing Mills................... 2
Cigar Box Makers................. 1	Plow Manufacturers............. 1
Cigars, Tobacco, etc................17	Plumbers and Gas Fitters........... 3
Clothing 8	Printing Houses................ 9
Coal and Wood................ 8	Pump Manufacturers............. 1
Collar Makers................ 2	Railways................ 5
Cotton Batting Makers............ 1	Real Estate Agents................11
Commission Merchants............ 7	Restaurants........................ 6
Contractors and Builders............ 6	Sugar Works................ 1
Confectionery.................. 6	Saddletree Makers. 2
Coopers 4	Saloons........................48
Coppersmiths 3	Saw Mills................ 1
Dentists.................. 6	Second-hand Goods........13
Drugs and Medicines..............13	Sewing Machine Offices............ 6
Dry Goods................. 8	Soap Manufacturers............ 2
Dyers................... 2	Sodawater Factories............. 2
Elevators................... 2	Stoves and Tinware................ 8
Engravers................. 3	Tailor Shops................15
Engravers and Silver Platers......... 2	Telegraph Companies............ 3
Express Offices 2	Telephone Companies........... 1
Flouring Mills.................. 4	Toys and Fancy Goods............. 3
Foundries, Iron................. 3	Trunk Makers................. 3
Fruits and Confectionery........12	Undertakers................ 3
Furniture Factories.............. 3	Veterinary Surgeons............. 2
Furniture Dealers................14	Vinegar Manufacturers............. 2
Grain Dealers................. 8	Wall Paper, etc................ 4
Gas Works................ 1	Watchmakers, Jewelers, etc........ 8
Groceries and Provisions............88	Woolen Mills................ 1

❖INDEX❖

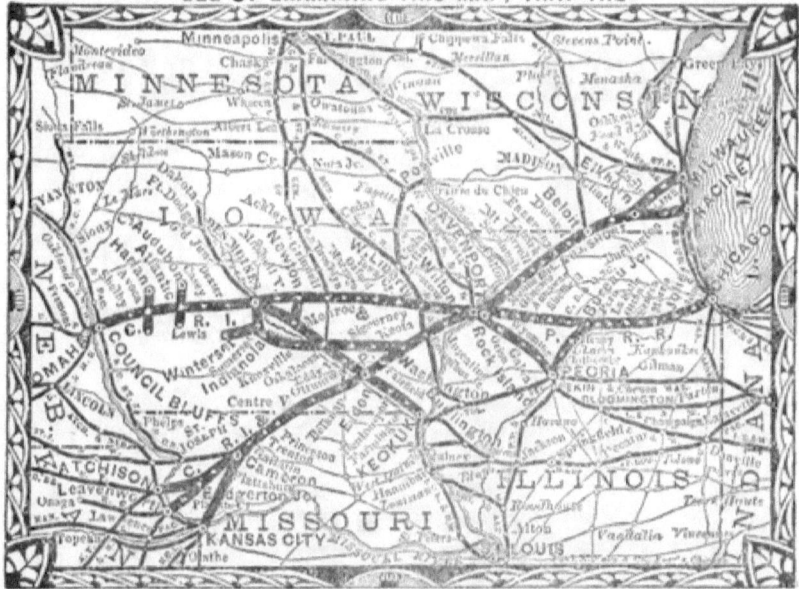

CHICAGO, BURLINGTON & QUINCY RAILROAD.

Take the BURLINGTON ROUTE, and find Traveling a Luxury instead of a Discomfort.

The CHICAGO, BURLINGTON & QUINCY DINING CARS, built by the Pullman Company expressly for this Line, are provided with all the latest improvements necessary to make them

ATTRACTIVE AND COMFORTABLE.

These Cars are used for no other purpose, and are always kept neat and clean·

The table is looked after by an experienced Caterer, and provided with

EVERY LUXURY OF THE SEASON,

And the service is of the best, while the charge is no greater than at the usual Eating Station,

SEVENTY-FIVE CENTS PER MEAL.

CENTRAL IOWA RAILWAY.

Short Route between Minnesota and all points South, East and West.

This line connects with the St. Louis, Kansas City & Northern Railway, and traverses the agricultural heart of Iowa — North and South. Pullman Sleeping Cars are run through daily between St. Louis, St. Paul and Minneapolis, *via* this line: the St. Louis, Kansas City & Northern, and the Chicago, Milwaukee & St. Paul Railways.

THE CONNECTIONS MADE ARE AS FOLLOWS:

1st.—With St. Paul & Pacific. 2d.—With Chicago, St. Paul & Minnesota Railways. 3rd.—With Illinois Central. 4th.—With Chicago & Northwestern R. R. 5th—With Chicago Rock Island & Pacific, and Grinnell & Montezuma Railroads. 6th.—With Chicago, Rock Island & Pacific Railroad. 7th.—With Chicago, Burlington & Quincy; Toledo, Peoria & Warsaw, and Indiana, Bloomington & Western Railways 8th.—With Chicago, Rock Island & Pacific Railroad; St. Louis, Kansas City & Northern Railroad and Chicago, Burlington & Quincy Railroad. 9th.—With Wabash, and Chicago, Rock Island & Pacific Railroads.

In brief, it makes close connections with all East and West trunk lines between St. Paul, Minnesota, and St. Louis, Missouri, and is the shortest and most popular route to the summer resorts of the North.

The main office of the Company is at Marshalltown, Iowa.

ISAAC M. CATE, President; D. N. PICKERING, Superintendent; C. A. JEWETT, Gen. P. T. & F. Agent; R. S. McMURRAY, Asst. Gen. T. Agent

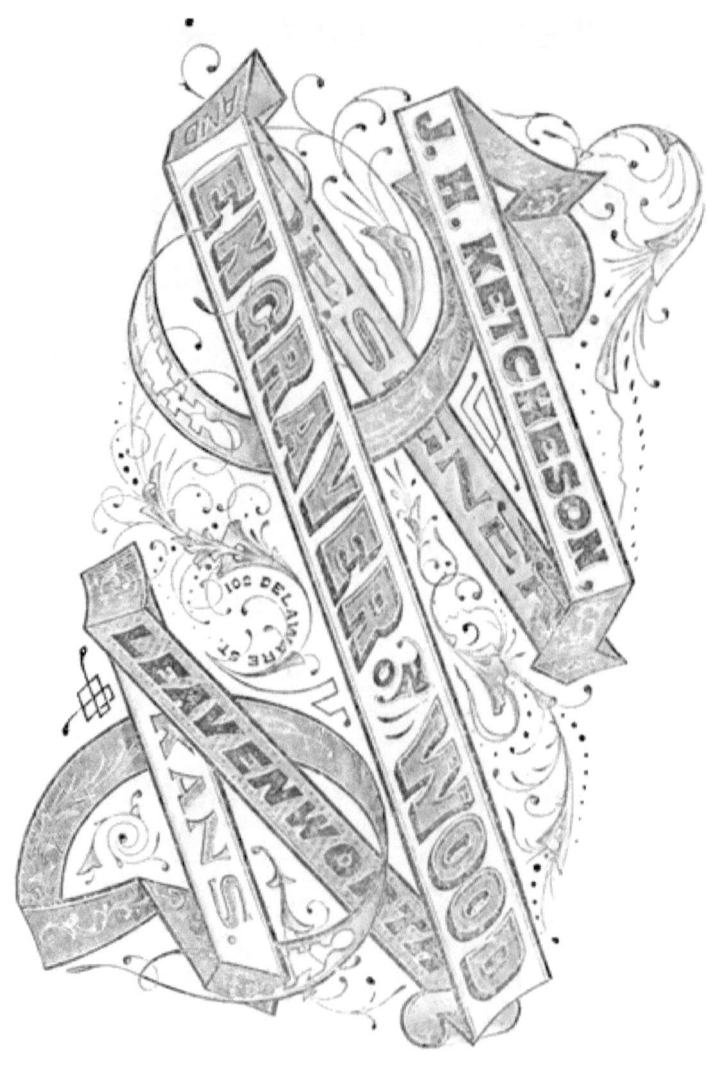

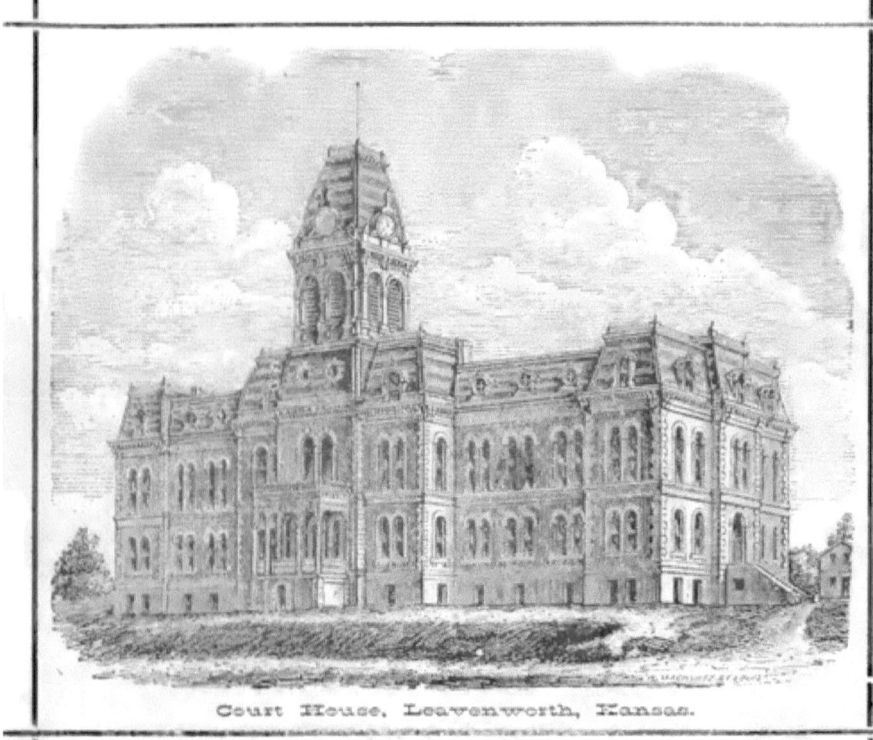
Court House, Leavenworth, Kansas.

Compliments of
Wesher Schussman
to the next President

www.ingramcontent.com/pod-product-compliance
Lightning Source LLC
Chambersburg PA
CBHW032204010726
47493CB00008BA/2828